FROM THE
NANCY DREW FILES

THE CASE: A toxic avenger targets TV st Brock
Sawyer at Oakwood Inn's Chocolate Fest   l.

CONTACT: Samantha Patton is in charge of   fes-
tivities— and Nancy's in charge of finding   set
out to poison Sam's ex-boyfriend, Brock.

SUSPECTS: Tim Krueger—Samantha's current oy-
friend sees red every time he sees Brock.

Jake Tagley—Samantha's stepbrother resent his
sister for having all the fun while he does al the
work.

Dan Avery—The sleazy photographer would do
anything for a hot story . . . even if he has to
the fire himself.

COMPLICATIONS: Nancy's   n-
  a is innocent—until   at
  nt Brock to the hospi

Books in the Nancy Drew Files ™ Series

THE NANCY DREW FILES™

Case 61
SWEET REVENGE

CAROLYN KEENE

AN ARCHWAY PAPERBACK
Published by SIMON & SCHUSTER
New York   London   Toronto   Sydney   Tokyo   Singapore

An Archway paperback
first published in Great Britain
by Simon & Schuster Ltd in 1994
A Paramount Communications Company

Simon & Schuster Ltd
West Garden Place
Kendal Street
London W2 2AQ

Simon & Schuster of Australia Pty Ltd
Sydney

A CIP catalogue record for this book is
available from the British Library

ISBN 0-671-85137-3

Printed and bound in Great Britain by
Harper*Collins* Manufacturing, Glasgow

SWEET REVENGE

Chapter

One

"WHEN ARE WE going to be there, Nan?"

Nancy Drew looked in the rearview mirror at her friend Bess Marvin, who was sitting in the back seat. Bess's blond hair was blowing back from her face in the warm summer breeze.

"We've still got another hour or so," Nancy said. She tucked a flyaway strand of reddish blond hair behind her ear. The two front windows were down all the way, and with the wind gusting, Nancy was glad she'd thought to pull her hair back in a French braid. Her friend, George Fayne, in the seat next to her, wore her hair short and had no trouble.

"Right," Bess said with a sigh. "It's just that— well, you guys know what I'm like around *one* chocolate dessert. The thought that I'm about to eat *thousands* of them is driving me crazy!"

"Not thousands, Bess," Nancy replied. "The Oakwood Inn brochure just said there'd be—"

"You don't have to tell me," interrupted Bess. "I've memorized the whole thing. 'Dozens of delectable chocolate creations for breakfast, lunch, and dinner, prepared by one of the state's most renowned pastry chefs,'" she parroted. "*And* cooking classes. *And* free samples." Bess's blue eyes sparkled at the thought. "It's a dream vacation, you guys. I just wish it would hurry up and start."

Almost a year had passed since Nancy had received the Oakwood Inn brochure advertising the Chocolate Festival. It sounded like so much fun that she had made reservations for the three of them right away.

They were all pretty different, Nancy reflected. Bess was curvy and blond and hated anything athletic and loved everything having to do with cute guys. George, with her short dark curls and lithe, athletic figure, liked guys, of course, but sports were high on her list of priorities, too. Nancy guessed that she fell somewhere in between, with her main loves being Ned Nickerson and a good mystery. The one thing that they *all* loved was chocolate, though.

"I'm amazed we were able to take this trip at all, Nancy," George observed. "I was sure you'd get called away on a case."

"*I* was sure she'd get called away by Ned," Bess added with a giggle.

Nancy was a detective, and the past couple of months had been unusually busy ones for her. Not only had she been practically blown up

2

during her last case, which she called *Poison Pen,* but Ned had also been home from college on vacation.

"It's only July, so I'll still be able to spend lots of time with Ned before he goes back to Emerson for the fall semester. Anyway, I'm sure the Chocolate Festival will take my mind off missing him for a few days."

"Chocolate has a way of doing that," Bess agreed. "But I hope there are at least one or two cute guys at the inn to take *my* mind off the desserts. I mean, I don't want to turn into a total blimp while I'm there."

"Okay, Bess, you can unpack your fork now," Nancy teased, turning the car into a long, sweeping driveway. "We're here!"

"This is an inn?" Bess asked in surprise. "I was expecting a little cottage. This place is huge!"

Bess was right, Nancy thought. The Oakwood Inn was a rambling four-story stone estate whose central building was flanked by two wings. Carefully tended flower beds lined the building, and the banner hanging over the door had the image of a slice of chocolate layer cake on it.

Nancy steered the Mustang into the parking lot, which was almost empty, and the three girls climbed out and began lugging their suitcases up the front walk toward the inn's wide front door. Just as Nancy was reaching for the door handle, she heard a voice behind her.

"Hey, wait! Let me give you a hand!"

Turning, Nancy saw a young man racing toward them. He looked about twenty years old. His sandy hair was falling into his hazel eyes, and he was dressed casually in a blue workshirt, jeans, and heavy workboots.

"I wonder where my stepsister is? *She's* supposed to be meeting the guests!" the guy said in a slightly annoyed tone. "I just came over from the other wing, where I was working, and happened to see you."

"Well, it's great of you to help us," Bess said quickly. She gave him a dazzling smile and tossed her long blond hair back over her shoulder. "We appreciate it."

Behind Bess, Nancy exchanged an amused look with George. Three minutes was the average time it took Bess to get a crush on someone. She was ahead of schedule that day.

The young man smiled back at Bess as he reached for her suitcase. "My name's Jake Tagley," he said. "I take it you three have come for the Chocolate Festival." He used his foot to push the front door open. "You're a little early, but—"

Jake didn't get to finish his sentence. Just as he was ushering Nancy, Bess, and George through the door, a beautiful girl rushed up to them and spoke. She was petite, with a waist-length mane of wavy black hair and huge dark eyes. Nancy guessed that she wasn't more than twenty-two or twenty-three, but she was dressed in a conservative navy skirt and blazer that made her look older.

"Jake! What are you doing here?" she asked angrily, trying without success to shuffle an armful of papers into order as she spoke to him. "I thought you were supposed to be putting down that new subfloor in the east wing!"

Jake set the suitcases down. "And I thought *you* were supposed to be meeting our guests," he snapped back. "If I hadn't noticed them, they'd probably still be trying to get through the door."

"Oh, no!" The girl's expression changed instantly from one of anger to dismay. Turning to Nancy and her friends, she said, "Oh, I'm so sorry! I was in my office! I didn't think anyone would get here until eleven!"

Nancy, Bess, and George introduced themselves, and the dark-haired girl said, "I'm Samantha Patton. I run the inn. I'm Jake's stepsister, and I'm also the director of the Chocolate Festival." She sighed ruefully. "Sorry I bit your head off like that, Jake. I guess I'm a little flustered."

"No problem," said Jake. "I know things are tense—and speaking of tension, where's Brock?"

Was it just Nancy's imagination, or did Samantha blush at her stepbrother's words? "He's—he's in my office, actually," Samantha said. She looked back over her shoulder at an open door down a hallway off the lobby. "We've been going over his schedule."

"His schedule," Jake echoed in a dubious tone. "I see."

Facing her stepbrother, Samantha said defiantly, "Oh, stop. It's not like that, and you know it."

"Let's just hope *Tim* knows it," was Jake's curt answer. "Now, as long as I'm here, why don't I show these young ladies to their rooms? Then I'll go back to work. Let me just get your keys. Marvin, Drew, and Fayne, right?"

"Right," Nancy confirmed. "But really, we can find our rooms ourselves if you're busy—"

"Oh, it's no trouble at all!" Jake called, smiling at Bess again. "I'm happy to help." He crossed the carpeted lobby to the front desk, a gleaming oak counter that curved in a semicircle against the far wall.

Nancy noted that hallways stretched back on either side of the desk, and open double doors led to a living room that ran along one-half of the front of the house. Damask armchairs and a sofa were set up by a fireplace on the wall opposite the living room. A wide hall opened up next to them, going back into what looked like a dining room. The place was homey and comfortable and just a little shabby. The sofa and chairs around the fireplace were frayed, and the lobby walls could have used a fresh coat of paint.

As though she had read Nancy's mind, Samantha said quickly, "We're doing a lot of renovations. We've got a long way to go, but the place is really going to be spectacular when it's finished. Oh—here's my mother!"

A tall, stately woman with steel gray hair swept back in a chignon was walking down the hall toward them.

"Samantha, have you checked that purchase

order for— Oh, excuse me." Samantha's mother broke off. "I didn't realize you had company."

"Yes, our first guests have arrived," said Samantha, a trifle nervously, Nancy thought. "Girls, this is my mother, Mrs. Tagley."

"It's a pleasure to meet you," said Mrs. Tagley. Her voice, like her smile, was formal and a bit frosty. "My husband is around somewhere. Pete?" she called down the hall she had just entered from.

After a second a shy-looking man about fifty-five emerged from a room down the hall and wandered out to the lobby. From his resemblance to Jake, it was clear that he was Jake's father. Like his son, he was wearing work clothes and heavy boots. He wiped his palm on his shirt before extending his hand to the girls. "Sawdust," he explained with an apologetic smile.

But Mrs. Tagley wasn't smiling. "Shouldn't you change into a coat and tie, dear?" she asked. Her tone of voice made it sound like an order, not a question.

Samantha said quickly, "Here's Jake with your keys, girls." Obviously she was trying to distract them from the exchange between her mother and stepfather. "I'll see you soon and show you around!" Then she dashed off down the hall.

Jake slung the girls' suitcases onto a cart, which he pushed down a hall lined with faded old portraits. "You're on the third floor," he said as Nancy, Bess, and George followed along.

As he pushed the elevator button for them,

Bess asked, "Could that Brock you were talking about back there possibly be Brock Sawyer?"

"Oh, you heard?" Jake said. "Yes, Brock Sawyer is definitely here."

"I thought that was who you might mean, but I couldn't believe it!" Bess marveled.

"Wow!" Even George was impressed. "He's just about the most famous TV actor in the country!"

"And definitely the cutest," Bess chimed in excitedly. "I usually hate cop shows, but 'City Heat' is the best show I've ever seen—and it's all because of Brock! Oh, I can't believe he's here!"

"How did Brock hear about the Chocolate Festival?" Nancy asked as the wooden elevator door creaked open. The Oakwood Inn didn't seem like the place a major TV star would spend his time.

"He's a—well, you might say, a friend of Samantha's," Jake said. He pressed the button for the third floor, and the elevator began its creaky ascent.

Bess's face fell. "How did she meet him?"

"It was a couple of years ago, before Brock made it big. He was in summer stock at a theater near Oakwood, and he and Samantha met at a cast party here at the inn. They hit it off right away."

"So I guess he's off-limits, right?" Bess asked.

"Not necessarily," Jake replied after a brief pause. "He and Samantha broke up at the end of that summer. She's got a new boyfriend now. His name's Tim Krueger, who's working for us as an accountant. But just between you and me," Jake went on, glancing meaningfully at the girls, "I don't think the flame between Sam and Brock is completely out."

"Well, don't give up hope," Bess said cheerfully, but it was clear to Nancy that what Bess was hoping for *wasn't* for Brock and Samantha to get back together.

When the elevator door slid open on the third floor, Jake showed the girls to their suite and deposited their bags inside the door. "The schedule of events for the festival is on the coffee table. See you later—I hope," he added, and closed the door quietly behind him.

The girls' rooms were comfortable but a bit threadbare. The three bedrooms adjoining the living room were too small to hold more than a bed and a dresser each. The living room carpet was worn in patches, and some of the tiles on the floor of the tiny bathroom were missing. But the gilt-wrapped box of handmade chocolates on the coffee table in the living room was certainly elegant, and the truffles were the best Nancy had ever tasted.

"This is going to be fun," George said as she stretched out in one of the living room's easy chairs and surveyed the box of chocolates with interest.

"Of course it's going to be fun," said Bess, her mouth already full of chocolate. "Hey, do you think I look good enough to meet Brock Sawyer?"

"Hang on a minute, Bess," George said cautiously. "If you're planning to act like some kind of crazed fan all weekend, I don't want to be seen in public with you."

"Of course I'm not!" Bess told her indignantly. "That would be totally uncool. Famous people hate it if you gush all over them. I just want to look nice in case we happen to bump into Brock, that's all. Nothing obvious."

Nancy picked up her suitcase and carried it into her bedroom. "Come on, then," she called back to Bess. "Let's get out of here before you eat that whole box of candy and can't get into any of your clothes."

The girls unpacked quickly, then headed back downstairs. The lobby was almost crowded now. Festival guests had obviously started to arrive, and they were milling around, waiting for information or the keys to their rooms.

"I bet Samantha's too busy to show us around now," said Nancy. "Maybe we could—"

"Nancy! George! Look over there!"

Bess's blue eyes were wide, and she was pointing a shaky finger down the wide hall. Samantha Patton was standing in a doorway. Next to her was a man all three girls recognized instantly.

Brock Sawyer was even more handsome in person than on TV, Nancy decided. Tall and slim, he had craggy features, wavy brown hair, and amazingly blue eyes—eyes that were fixed on Samantha.

"It's him! It's him!" Bess's whisper was more like a scream, and several people in the lobby turned to look. "I've got to go get his autograph!

I've got to meet him! I've got to— Wait here!"
Before the girls could stop her, Bess was dashing
toward Samantha and Brock Sawyer, jostling
other guests as she raced by.

"Nothing obvious, eh?" George murmured,
rolling her eyes. "Brother!"

Just as Bess rushed over to Samantha and
Brock, two things happened. The first was that
Brock leaned down and slipped his arm around
Samantha's shoulders.

Nancy's head swiveled automatically toward
Bess. That was when she saw the second thing.
From out of nowhere a young man with dark
brown hair and icy green eyes raced up behind
Bess, shoved her out of the way, and aimed a
vicious punch at Brock's jaw.

Chapter

Two

Y OU KEEP AWAY from Samantha!" the young man yelled as he threw the punch.

Brock Sawyer ducked just in time, and the young man's fist crashed into the doorjamb. Nancy noticed that Bess had halted a few feet from them, a startled expression on her face.

"Tim, what's your problem?" Samantha shouted angrily. "Stop it!"

So that angry blond guy was Tim Krueger, Samantha's boyfriend, Nancy realized. He was obviously very upset about Brock. Ignoring Samantha, he reeled backward and began swinging at Brock again.

"No, Tim!" Samantha cried. "Please, somebody stop him!"

"*I'll* stop him," Brock growled between

12

clenched teeth—and he slugged Tim right in the stomach.

Nancy grimaced as Tim doubled over. Behind her a woman let out a frightened gasp.

What can I do to stop this? Nancy thought.

She scanned the crowd, and for a second her gaze landed on a short, heavyset man standing beside the fireplace. He had a camera up to his face and was busily snapping picture after picture of the fight.

Ugh! Nancy thought. What a nasty way to behave! A grunt from Tim brought her thoughts back to the fight.

Tim was lurching unsteadily forward, ready to throw another punch. Nancy started forward to grab him. Then, from somewhere in the crowd, Jake Tagley stepped around Nancy.

"That's enough, guys," he said, stepping firmly between Tim and Brock. With a swift movement of his arms he pushed the two men apart.

Gasping for breath, Brock and Tim glared murderously at each other. A hush had fallen on the guests in the lobby. Then the silence was broken.

"Are—are you all right, Mr. Sawyer?" came Bess's hesitant voice.

"I'm fine," Brock Sawyer answered, scowling. "It would take more than this to—"

"Then may I have your autograph?" Bess interrupted.

Everyone in the lobby burst into laughter.

A reluctant grin spread across Brock Sawyer's face, too. "Let me just ask the boss," he answered with a nod toward Samantha. "You're the one who's been keeping track of my schedule, Sam. Do I have time?"

"Uh, sure, Brock. This would be a good time for me to check in with the kitchen. I want to see how everything's coming along." Nancy noticed that Samantha was shaking slightly.

"I can check for you," offered Tim. From his expression Nancy guessed he wanted to smooth things over.

But Samantha wasn't about to let him off easy. Giving him a frosty glare, she snapped, "No, thanks. You've done enough already."

Then suddenly she seemed to remember the guests and turned to face them. "Sorry about the disturbance, folks!" she called, her voice full of forced cheer. "Why don't you come over and meet our celebrity guest? And don't forget to be at the Round Room at twelve-thirty for the first chocolate event of the day. Lunch will be at one-thirty in the dining room."

Samantha's words broke the last of the tension in the room. More than a dozen people crowded around Brock, all talking at once. Brock, too, had become the professional once again. He was smiling and chatting easily as he signed the scraps of paper people were holding out to him.

In the commotion the people in the crowd seemed to have forgotten the fight. All but Tim, who was leaning against the wall, scrutinizing Brock with flashing green eyes. Next to Tim, Jake was bending down to pick up his toolbox.

"Want to give me a hand in the east wing?" Nancy heard him ask Tim quietly.

Tim opened his mouth to say something, then seemed to think better of it. Raking a hand through his hair, he shrugged and then followed Jake out the door.

"Looks like we've got all the makings of a good soap opera here," George said into Nancy's ear.

"Apparently, some of the other guests think so, too," Nancy whispered back. She flicked a thumb toward the fireplace. "See that guy with the camera over there? He was taking pictures during the whole fight."

George followed Nancy's gaze. "Press, probably," she suggested.

"Maybe. He's not wearing a press badge, though. I'm going to head over there to see what he's up to."

"Always the detective," said George, laughing. "I'll wait here for Bess."

Nancy was frowning when she came back ten minutes later.

"So, what's his story?" George asked.

"The guy's name is Dan Avery. Apparently, he's just a nut for chocolate, like the rest of us," Nancy explained. "But—I don't know. All that camera equipment he's got looks a lot more expensive than most people would carry around, and—"

"Hey," said Bess, rushing up to them and waving a cocktail napkin. "Look at my autograph. Let's hang around until the crowd thins

15

out a little. Maybe we'll get a chance to really talk to Brock."

"Come *on*, Bess," George said with a groan.

"He'll be here all weekend," Nancy added, "All we've seen so far is the lobby, and I'd like to check out the inn a little."

Reluctantly Bess followed her friends. "Some people don't recognize *real* scenery when they see it," she grumbled under her breath.

"Hey, George! I found an antique!" Bess called from a corner of the torn-up room that the girls were exploring. She held up a creased wall map. "What do you think it's worth?"

The girls had made their way up a flight of stairs into the east wing. This was the part of the inn being worked on, and the girls had gotten dirt and sawdust all over their clothes.

"Ten cents, probably," George told her cousin with a grin. "But look at this!" She showed Nancy and Bess a tiny porcelain figurine she had found on the dusty mantelpiece. "If someone cleaned this up, it would be really pretty."

Nancy glanced around the room. It had a forlorn, abandoned quality, as did the other east wing rooms they'd been in. They had poked through bedrooms with four-poster beds wearing canopies of cobwebs, and bathrooms with shelves lined with long-forgotten brands of shampoo and soap. Except for the areas under construction, the east wing looked as though it hadn't been visited in about fifty years.

"There's lots of stuff here that would look nice

16

if someone cleaned it up," Nancy commented. She brushed her hands together to get rid of some dust. "They must have left the whole east wing pretty much the way it was when they closed it off."

Bess shivered nervously. "I feel as though we're surrounded by ghosts, don't you?"

"Nope," said George cheerfully. "Let's go check out some more rooms."

Suddenly Bess froze. "Wait!" she whispered. "What's that bumping sound?"

Nancy stuck her head out into the hallway. "It's just Jake," she said, catching sight of his sandy hair and jeans. "Hi, Jake!"

He was walking down the hallway toward them, lugging a power saw. "Find any skeletons yet?" he asked.

"Not yet," Nancy told him, "but this sure looks like the kind of place where we could."

"You're right," Jake agreed. "In a few months, though, you won't recognize this place. If you can believe it, we're actually about to finish one of the rooms in this wing—the new conference room. It should be done today."

"You must have been working hard getting ready for this weekend," Bess observed.

"We've been going pretty much nonstop for the past few months," Jake replied, nodding. "Tim helps when he can, but he's pretty busy with his own job."

"Your dad's been helping, too, right?" asked George, wiping her hands on her shorts.

"Yes. But mostly he works in the basement,"

Jake told her. "He's building bookcases in his workshop. My dad's really a cabinetmaker, not a carpenter.

"In fact, that's how he met my stepmother," Jake went on. "He was hired to do some restoration work a few years ago. Samantha's mother was running the inn then, too. She and my father hit it off, and they got married about six months later."

"That's so romantic!" Bess exclaimed. "Love at first sight!"

"Well, maybe," said Jake slowly. "I'm not sure it was the greatest match, but—" Suddenly he broke off. "It's none of my business as long as my dad's happy, I guess."

Bess seemed not to notice his doubtful tone. "This inn would be a great setting for a romance," she said. "Though not the east wing, of course."

"I guess not," Jake agreed ruefully.

"So Mrs. Tagley was running the inn alone before?" Nancy asked, half to herself.

"Right," Jake said with a nod. "She took it over after her first husband died. I don't know much about him, but there are people on the staff who were here even before my stepmother came. I hear her first husband was a nice enough guy, but she was really the one in charge. Kind of like now."

"But I thought Samantha ran the inn now," George put in.

"Well, she's certainly on her way," Jake said proudly. "Sam graduated from hotel school last year at the top of her class. The Chocolate Festival was her idea. Her mother has always been a great pastry chef and candy maker, so Samantha decided to use those talents to promote the inn. We've been trying to come up with ways to bring in more people, and—"

He stopped again, and a deep blush crept over his face. "Guess I've been working by myself too long," he said awkwardly. "I'm really rambling on. Sorry."

"Hey, we don't mind," Nancy said quickly. "This place looks like it has so much history. It's nice to learn some of it. Do you work here full time?"

"Oh, no. I'm in hotel school, too. Once I saw the possibilities for this place, I got bitten by the same bug as Samantha and my stepmother. I'm still in my first year, though. What about you three?" he went on. "No fair for me to answer all the questions. Are you students or chefs or what? What brings you to our little chocolate paradise?"

"Love of chocolate, plain and simple," said Nancy with a smile.

"That's right," Bess echoed. "Nancy's a detective. But the only mystery she's going to be solving this weekend is how I'm going to fit into my clothes after all the chocolate I plan to eat."

"Speaking of chocolate," George put in, checking her watch, "weren't we supposed to be somewhere at twelve-thirty? It's twelve twenty-five now."

"That's right!" said Bess. "The Round Room,

our schedule said. Jake, could you tell us how to get there?"

A wide smile spread over Jake's face. "I'll do better than that. I'll take you there myself," he told the girls. "Just give me a second to brush off all the sawdust."

"So this is the Round Room," commented a woman walking through the door ahead of Nancy, Bess, and George. They all stopped to take the pieces of paper and pencils being handed to them. "Well, it fits its name."

She was right. The Round Room was certainly round—a white, windowless room that made Nancy feel as though she were standing inside a huge drum. It was filled with expectant and hungry people.

"Mmm." Bess gave a rapturous sniff and grabbed George's arm as she made it into the room. "What's that incredible smell?"

"That," said Samantha, who happened to be standing nearby, "is melted chocolate. Pure, rich Creamfield's milk chocolate. Three hundred pounds of it. See that vat over there?" She pointed to an immense copper kettle standing on a platform at one end of the room, a dark green silk curtain behind it, setting the copper off perfectly. "It's full of melted chocolate."

"Great, but what's it for?" asked George.

Samantha laughed, and Nancy was glad to see she'd shaken off her bad mood after the fight between Tim and Brock. "It's designed to tempt you into buying Creamfield's milk chocolate, of course. They're bringing out a new line of super-deluxe candy bars that weigh a pound apiece. Some Creamfield's executive got the idea that the best way to promote the new chocolate was to let people smell it. And since melted chocolate smells even better than *un*melted chocolate, they send that dipping vat filled with chocolate around to festivals like this one."

Samantha gave them a tempting smile. "Hurry on up front so you'll get a good view. You might get a chance to win a couple hundred Creamfield's chocolate bars, if you're lucky."

"How?" Bess asked.

Samantha just raised her eyebrows mysteriously. "You'll find out."

The girls followed Samantha as she threaded her way through the crowd toward the platform that held the vat of melted chocolate. They found a place at the front and watched Samantha jump up onto the platform, pick up a microphone, and move over to the vat of chocolate.

"Attention, please, chocolate lovers!" Samantha said brightly. "Welcome to Oakwood Inn's first annual Chocolate Festival!"

Loud applause rang out from around the room.

"We'd like to kick off the festival with a little contest," Samantha announced. "To help us, please welcome the festival's celebrity taster, Mr. Brock Sawyer!"

Beaming, Brock strode up onto the stage and put his arm around Samantha. Nancy couldn't help but notice Tim, who was slouching against the curved wall. He looked pretty miserable. His fists were slightly clenched, and the expression on his face was drawn and tight.

"And the prize," Samantha went on, "is the next best thing to Brock himself—Brock's weight in Creamfield chocolate bars!"

With a flourish she pulled open the green curtain behind them to reveal what looked like a mountain of chunky chocolate bars. They were piled high next to a huge, old-fashioned scale that hung suspended from the ceiling.

"We're going to ask Brock to climb onto one side of this scale," explained Samantha. "And then we're going to ask you to guess how many delicious Creamfield's chocolate bars it will take to equal Brock's weight. Whoever guesses correctly wins all the chocolate. Please fill out your papers and put them in this box on the stage." When the last guess was tucked inside, she said, "Okay, here goes!"

There was a buzz of excitement from the audience as Brock, with a wave of mock farewell at the audience, climbed carefully onto one side of the huge scale and perched gingerly in the pan.

"It's kind of an unsteady perch," Samantha said, "so I'm going to use these straps to keep Brock from sliding off."

"Oh, I wish I'd brought my camera," moaned Bess softly.

Lots of other guests had brought theirs. They were crowding forward now to snap the comical picture Brock made wobbling around on the huge scale. Nancy noticed that Dan Avery had made his way to the front with his camera. He was kneeling on the ground just in front of Nancy, snapping away.

"Now let's hear what some of your guesses were!" called Samantha. She pointed to a woman across the room from Nancy. "Yes, ma'am?"

"A hundred and sixty-two!"

"Okay," said Samantha. "Let's try it."

She picked up handfuls of the large candy bars and piled them on the scale.

"Hey, wait a second. The scale's tipping!" Brock exclaimed.

Nancy's attention snapped to the actor. "It's doing more than that!" she added. "It's shaking!"

Brock grabbed at the edge of the pan to steady himself, but the shaking only grew worse.

"I've got to get off this thing!" he shouted, pulling at the straps tying him to the scale.

But it was too late. With a tremendous crash the scale tipped forward. Brock soared through the air—and landed headfirst in the vat of steaming melted chocolate!

Chapter
Three

OH, NO! He'll be boiled to death!" shrieked Bess.

"That's impossible," said a thin, bespectacled man near her. "Fine chocolate is never heated to the boiling point. The cocoa butter would—"

Nancy didn't bother listening to the rest. She leapt onto the stage just as Brock's head appeared above the edge of the tempering pot. He was coughing, sputtering, and trying unsuccessfully to wipe chocolate from his face with a chocolate-drenched hand.

Samantha reached the pot at the same time as Nancy, and both girls held down their hands to Brock. "Are you all right?" Samantha cried.

"I—I think I am," sputtered Brock.

By this time both Tim and Jake had also rushed forward to help. The four of them tugged on Brock's hands and arms. As they were yanking him over the edge of the vat, it unexpectedly tipped.

Nancy jumped back, but there was no avoiding the wave of hot melted chocolate that cascaded onto her feet, covering the stage and dripping down to the floor. Brock, Samantha, Tim, and Jake—all of them as chocolate-covered as Nancy—were unable to move. The guests who were closest to the stage yelped and stepped hastily back.

Except for one—Dan Avery. He pushed his way through the crowd so eagerly that for a second Nancy almost thought he wanted to lap up some of the melted chocolate. Once he was near the stage, though, he held up his camera and began taking pictures.

"What is that guy's problem?" Nancy heard George say to Bess. And next to her, a disgusted-looking Brock was trying to wipe chocolate from his face. "I've got to get to a shower," he muttered.

"Right away," Samantha agreed. She turned to Tim and Jake. "Could you guys do me a big favor and start cleaning up this mess while I help Brock to his room? I'll help later."

"Sure thing," said Jake.

"I really appreciate it," said Samantha. Then she turned toward the guests. "Sorry, folks," she said with a strained smile. "We didn't mean to go quite so far to get your attention. I guess we'll have to postpone this contest—but don't despair. In an hour we'll be serving the first of our spectacular Chocolate Festival meals—complete with a surprise dessert."

"Haven't we had enough surprises for one day?" a woman remarked tartly. "First we get ringside seats at a boxing match. Then we get dipped in chocolate! This isn't the most *festive* festival I've ever been to."

Samantha's mouth was set in a straight line, Nancy noticed. "Well, I'm sure things will go smoothly from now on," Samantha assured the crowd. "Now I'd better help poor Mr. Sawyer. Don't worry about getting chocolate on the floor, Brock. We can clean it up later."

As the guests began to trickle out of the room after Samantha, Nancy said, "I'm going to have to clean up, but first I'd like to get a closer look at that vat of chocolate."

"Fine," said George, who had remained untouched by the chocolate. "Maybe Bess and I will check out the grounds. We'll see you at one-thirty."

Stepping around Tim and Jake, who were scraping sticky chocolate off the platform, Nancy went over to the vat and scale. She was grateful that they didn't seem to notice her. They both seemed preoccupied with something Tim was muttering angrily about.

"Why did Samantha say she'd help us clean up the chocolate?" Tim was saying. "Because you know with one thing and another, she won't be able to help us. She'll have to check something in her office or make a phone call. Or talk to Brock," he finished in disgust.

"I know what you mean," Jake said sympathetically.

Nancy was listening with only half an ear. Her attention was mainly concentrated on the scale that had tipped Brock into the chocolate.

"What's so interesting about that scale?"

Suddenly Nancy realized that Jake's question was directed at her. "Oh, nothing," she replied casually. "I've just never seen one of these up close."

That was true, and up close Nancy could see that there was something wrong with it.

The two pans on either side of the scale were held up by chains that, in turn, were attached to one central chain. There seemed to be some kind of crack in one link of the chain leading to the pan Brock had been sitting on. Bending in to examine it even more carefully, she saw that the link had been filed almost all the way through!

Someone had *meant* that chain to loosen and stretch, which would dump the contents—Brock—into the vat. But who? And why?

There was no way to answer those questions before lunch, Nancy realized. She might as well get cleaned up.

Saying nothing about her discovery, Nancy murmured a quick "See you guys later," then walked out of the Round Room.

The inn was so big and rambling, she decided to try a new route back to the room. The hallway she chose was dimly lit and empty—except for Dan Avery, who was talking on a pay phone in a little alcove.

He was speaking so venomously that he didn't even notice Nancy as she walked past. "Absolutely. I'm in total control. Believe me, I'll take care of him for you. I'll get that actor if it's the last thing I do."

"Chocolate *rice?* I can't believe it!" Nancy exclaimed at lunch.

The Chocolate Festival's first lunch had just begun—and chocolate had made its way into every course. The rice served with the shrimp main course had unsweetened cocoa in it, though not enough to make it taste strange, Nancy was relieved to note. The butter served with the chocolate whole-wheat rolls was chocolate flavored. There was even chocolate salad dressing on the fruit salad.

"I can't imagine what dessert will be," Nancy said, scooping some rice onto her fork.

Brock Sawyer smiled down at her, his blue eyes sparkling. "I don't know, but you'd better save some room for it. It's bound to be delicious."

Before the meal Samantha had spotted Nancy, Bess, and George hesitating at one end of the dining room, trying to decide where to sit. She had asked them to join her family, Tim, and—to Bess's delight—Brock.

Now Nancy was feeling a little uncomfortable, though. Brock had spent most of the meal talking to her. She was seated between him and Samantha. Nancy kept trying to steer the conversation toward Bess, who was seated on Brock's other side, but it wasn't working.

Bess kept trying to steer the conversation in her direction, too. "Want some of this chocolate butter, Brock?" she asked eagerly. "It's great!"

"No, thanks, Bess. I'm watching my weight. With all the chocolate I have to taste here, I need to be careful the rest of the time. I had a long session with my nutritionist before I came, and she told me what I could and couldn't eat. I'm going to stick to her rules if it kills me."

He turned back to Nancy and went on with what he had been saying before. "I'm just glad that Samantha had the good sense to keep the tabloid reporters away from this festival. If there's anything I can't stand, it's those junky supermarket newspapers. They make up the worst lies I've ever read."

"Do they write about you a lot?" asked Nancy.

Brock grimaced. "Oh, yeah. The more successful 'City Heat' has gotten, the more they've picked on me. Especially the *Midnight Examiner*. The last time I saw an issue, they were claiming that I was married to my thirteen-year-old cousin. I don't even have any cousins. My fiasco in that chocolate vat would have been right up the *Examiner*'s alley."

Suddenly Mrs. Tagley leaned across the table. "And just what caused that disaster, Samantha?" she asked sharply.

"I don't know yet, Mom," Samantha replied in a tight voice. "I'll get on it, don't worry. There are a lot of other things at the inn that need my attention besides that."

Mrs. Tagley briefly patted her gray hair. "Well,

if you're going to be running this place, as you insist on doing, you have to be concerned with *everything*," she said evenly. "A good innkeeper keeps track of the details *and* the big picture, you know."

A sugary-sweet smile spread across Samantha's face. "All right, Mom," she cooed. "I'll just follow *your* good example, okay?"

Uh-oh, thought Nancy. That sounded like a direct jab at Mrs. Tagley's own innkeeping skills. From what Jake had said earlier, Oakwood had been having trouble attracting customers. Was Samantha implying that that had been her mother's fault?

Now Mrs. Tagley seemed as though she was about to explode, but her husband intervened.

"Let's leave this for another time, all right?" Mr. Tagley said quietly. He looked stiff and uncomfortable in his suit and tie. "The festival's driving us all crazy enough as it is. No need to bother our company with it, too."

"Oh, all right," snapped Mrs. Tagley.

This family certainly didn't seem to be self-conscious about arguing in front of total strangers! Nancy thought.

She decided it was time to try to get people back into a good mood. "This is a fantastic meal," she told Mrs. Tagley. "I can't believe your chef could prepare chocolate in so many interesting ways."

"Wait till you taste dessert," Jake volunteered. He sounded relieved at the change of subject.

"My stepmother's chocolate desserts are out of this world. They're the thing that's kept this inn going for the past couple of years."

Once again he broke off, embarrassed, and nervously brushed his sandy hair back. Nancy guessed he hadn't meant to blurt out yet another reminder that the inn was in trouble.

"What *is* for dessert?" she asked swiftly.

"Brock Sawyer—the chocolate version, that is," Mrs. Tagley said mysteriously.

"What do you mean?" asked Bess.

"You'll have to see for yourself," Samantha put in. Glancing around at the other tables, she asked, "Do you think people are ready for dessert yet?"

"Definitely!" Bess and George said in unison.

"Well, then, I'll go get it!"

Samantha jumped up and walked across the dining room toward a cart by the kitchen door, where Nancy could see there was something covered with a white cloth on the cart. As Samantha wheeled the cart to the front of the room, conversation at the other tables began to die down.

"Did everyone have a nice lunch?" Samantha asked, smiling as the guests burst into applause.

"You couldn't possibly find room for more chocolate, could you?"

"Yes! Yes!" people called out.

"Then I guess we're just going to *have* to give you what you want. As some of you may know, my mother is a real artist with chocolate." Once again the room filled with applause. "And for dessert today, she's made what I think is her finest creation ever.

"I'm going to ask our special guest to unveil this spectacular dessert for us," Samantha went on. She glanced toward Nancy's table. "Ready, Brock?"

Smiling broadly, Brock stood and walked over to her. "Here goes!" he said. With a flourish he picked up a corner of the white cloth and whisked it off the dessert.

Then his smile turned into a shudder of disgust. "What *is* this?" he shouted.

Everyone craned their necks to see what he was talking about—and a confused murmur filled the room.

On the table was a spectacular white-chocolate cake—a replica of Brock's face. It was stunning, except for one thing.

The whole surface of the cake was pulsating with a living blanket of ants!

Chapter

Four

WHAT *IS* THIS, Samantha?" Rage and horror were mixed in Brock's voice, and Nancy couldn't blame him. She had seen few sights as bizarre and sickening.

Samantha drew a shaky breath and staggered backward a few steps. She looked as if she was about to faint, but her voice was steady as she summoned a waiter.

"Please take this back to the kitchen and dispose of it immediately." As the waiter gripped the cart and wheeled it away, Samantha returned to her seat, motioning for Brock to do the same. Once there, she beckoned to another waiter.

"Could you ask the chefs to put together another dessert immediately?"

"Another—another dessert?" the waiter faltered. "What kind, Miss Patton?"

"There's plenty of ice cream in the freezers, isn't there?" Jake suggested, coming to the rescue.

Samantha gratefully turned to her stepbrother. "Yes, and lots of fudge sauce. We can have sundaes."

Nodding, Jake jumped to his feet. "I'll go help in the kitchen. I'm sure they could use an extra hand."

The whole conversation had taken about thirty seconds. Glancing around, Nancy could tell that only the guests closest to the cake saw what had happened. But the people who *had* seen the ants had disgusted expressions on their faces.

"Darling, let's get out of here," Nancy heard a wan-looking woman at the next table say to her husband. "I feel sick." Her husband helped her to her feet, and they hurried out of the room.

Samantha stared bleakly at Nancy. "I sure am getting a lot of practice calming down guests," she commented. "I'd better fix things up." She stood up to address the crowd.

"They say bad things come in threes," she called cheerfully. Nancy and George exchanged an admiring glance. Samantha sounded unbelievably poised. "So I'm sure we'll have no more trouble from now on!

"I think you'll find that our replacement dessert will take your minds off anything unpleasant. You're just about to taste a good old-fashioned sundae made with homemade vanilla ice cream and my mother's fabulous ultra-fudge sauce. Here come the waiters now!"

She gestured toward some waiters carrying trays of sundaes through the kitchen door. Several "oohs" rose up from the diners.

"Let's hope that works," Samantha said under her breath, sinking back into her chair. "I'm not sure how much longer I can continue to smooth things over."

"I'm not sure, either," Brock Sawyer told her flatly. "I'm a pretty good actor, but it's getting hard to act as if I'm having a good time. I think it might be time for me to head back to California."

At Brock's words Nancy darted a quick glance around the table. Jake and Mr. Tagley seemed to be concerned, but to Nancy's surprise, Mrs. Tagley looked oddly happy. Why would she *want* to lose the festival's star? Brock's participation was a definite plus for the inn. If he left, the festival's reputation could suffer. Why would Mrs. Tagley be happy about something that might hurt the inn?

On the other hand, Nancy wasn't at all surprised to see that Tim was also pleased at Brock's words. He was eyeing Brock with an expression that seemed to say, So you can't handle it, huh?

"Brock, you can't go!" Samantha pleaded quietly, grasping his arm. "We need you here! Please promise you'll stay."

"Well—" Brock paused. "I really don't know—" Then he smiled at Samantha and put his hand over hers. "Maybe for a *little* longer— just to help a friend in need."

A waiter was hovering over his shoulder with a sundae in his hand, but Brock waved him away.

"Can't waste the calories," he explained. "I'd love some coffee, though."

As the waiter moved on, Brock explained to his dinner companions, "I brought my own low-cal sweetener—my nutritionist recommended it." He pulled out a small glass jar to show them. "Conscience, it's called. Great stuff."

"As he's told everyone in this inn since he got here," Tim grumbled under his breath. "Waiters included."

As the conversation began to pick up at their table, George leaned forward and spoke to Nancy in a low voice. "Aren't these accidents getting a little suspicious?"

"Definitely," Nancy whispered back. "As soon as lunch is over, I'm going to look around a little. Those ants didn't just find that cake. Someone put them there. If I'm lucky, I'll find a clue or two to tell me what happened."

"Can I help you, miss?"

Nancy looked up with a start from where she had been peering behind the refrigerator. A busboy had paused in the kitchen doorway, his arms full of dishes and a questioning expression on his face.

"Have you had problems with ants before today?" Nancy asked him.

The busboy shook his head. "You can't believe how clean this kitchen is," he said, stepping over to the counter and setting the dishes down with a clatter. "Mrs. Tagley is a real— I mean, everyone at the inn keeps an eye on the kitchen. The trash is taken out six times a day just so we don't attract any pests. Besides, how could ants crawl through tile walls and a tile floor?" he asked, then seemed to forget she was there.

No way that Nancy could think of. That made her more certain that someone had *brought* the ants into the kitchen. But in what?

She'd already checked under the steam tables and behind the huge glass-doored refrigerators. The shelves, with their neat rows of kitchen supplies, had turned up nothing. Nancy had even stirred through the industrial-size garbage cans at one end of the kitchen with no success. And now she was starting to worry that the kitchen staff would kick her out soon.

Nancy let out a sigh, brushed back her reddish blond hair, and started to leave, bumping into a stainless-steel worktable on the way. Then it occurred to her that she hadn't examined the rows of pots and pans under the huge worktables.

In the bottom of a two-gallon double boiler, Nancy found what she'd been looking for.

"An empty jar wrapped in an apron? Why are you showing me that, Nancy?" Samantha asked. She was staring blankly at the bundle Nancy had plopped down on the desk in her office.

"Look more closely," Nancy urged. "This is what held the ants we saw on the cake."

It was a large half-gallon glass jar. It had probably been a mayonnaise jar, Nancy thought, but there was no mayonnaise in it now. There were only ants—a few sluggish ones crawling sleepily around the bottom of the jar.

"I found it hidden in the kitchen," Nancy explained. "I think whoever put those ants on the cake brought them into the kitchen in this."

"But—but where would someone get ants?" Samantha asked, confusion in her dark eyes.

"That wouldn't be too hard," Nancy answered. "Some pet stores sell ants for ant farms. All anyone would have to do is put them in the refrigerator for a few minutes to make them sluggish enough to pour onto the—"

"Stop!" Samantha was turning slightly green. "I believe you," she said quickly. "But who would do something like that?"

"I don't know," Nancy admitted. "Maybe the same person who set up the scale so it would tip while Brock was being weighed."

Now Samantha was even more confused. "Set up the—the scale?"

"I forgot to tell you about that," Nancy said gravely. Quickly she filled Samantha in. "I don't know whether these pranks are being aimed at Brock or the festival in general," she finished. "But I'm a detective, and if you'd like me to investigate, I'd be happy to."

"*No!*" Samantha said emphatically. Then, as if to calm herself, she began rubbing her temples. "No, thank you, I mean. I'm sure these were just isolated incidents. The scale was probably already broken."

"But if someone's out to sabotage the festival or hurt Brock—"

"No, Nancy," Samantha said firmly. "That's impossible. It's—it's just an old mayonnaise jar, after all. I'll tell the kitchen staff to do a better job cleaning up from now on."

She seemed so determined not to hear Nancy's message that Nancy didn't bother pointing out that someone had already done an excellent cleanup job—on the jar. There wasn't a fingerprint on it.

"Pure cocoa butter," a woman with a round face and bouffant hairdo was telling Nancy. "That's the only way you can get it to melt properly. I buy mine from a mail-order place in Switzerland. Would you like the address?"

"It sounds wonderful, but I don't think so," Nancy said politely.

Dinner had just ended—a fabulous buffet that included everything from melon in white-chocolate sauce to turkey with chocolate stuffing to chocolate-raspberry mousse torte. Now Nancy, Bess, and George were in the living room—a cozy room with a flagstone fireplace at one end, and sofas and chairs scattered throughout—as they waited for the final chocolate event of the day.

The woman headed off to find someone else to trade recipes with, and Nancy turned to Bess. "I think the people here take chocolate even more seriously than you do, Bess."

39

"Impossible," Bess said promptly. "I mean, I've eaten about four thousand chocolate things today, and I still can't *wait* to try those new chocolate creams Samantha was telling us about."

"They did sound pretty scrumptious," George agreed.

At dinner Samantha had announced that Oakwood Inn was planning to launch a line of its own homemade chocolates. And Brock Sawyer was going to give the new chocolates their first official taste.

"I wonder how famous you have to be before you're asked to be a taste tester at one of these things," Bess said longingly. "Oh, look, there's Brock! I'll ask *him.*" She bolted across the room toward the actor.

Nancy chuckled. "Bess doesn't believe in playing hard to get, does she?" she said to George. "Let's go see how her tactics are working."

When they reached Bess, she was saying, "But don't you get full? I can't eat more than a bite of these rich desserts, myself."

George elbowed Nancy in the ribs, and Nancy had to bite her tongue to keep from laughing. But Brock seemed to buy Bess's act.

The actor shook some of his special artificial sweetener into a glass of iced tea he was holding and took a big swig. "I'm just grateful I've got such a great nutritionist," he told Bess. "If she hadn't told me about this sweetener, I'd be a total blimp, with all the sampling I'm supposed to be doing. But I admit I'm looking forward to sampling these chocolates."

Brock set his glass down on a coffee table. "At least I would be, if I were hungrier. That dinner did me in. I wonder if—"

"Ready, Brock?" Samantha spoke up from behind him. She was wearing a red dress that set off her dark hair, which fell in pretty waves down her back. In her hands was a gleaming red box tied with a silver ribbon.

"I sure am." Brock was a little pale, but his voice was resolute as he followed Samantha to the fireplace. "Nice talking to you, Bess."

As the girls squeezed into a love seat near the fireplace, Samantha held the red box aloft. "Ladies and gentlemen, your attention, please. I'd like you to meet my mother's newest candy— Silk and Cream Chocolates! They're really something—made with pure Wisconsin cream and imported Belgian chocolate, from a recipe formulated by my mother. Tomorrow Silk and Cream Chocolates will hit the stores, but tonight our star taster will enjoy the very first bite!"

Samantha handed the red box to Brock. "These are my own personal favorites—Lemon Mousse Truffles."

Brock pulled the ribbon open with a long, sweeping dramatic gesture. He reached in and lifted out a dark chocolate shaped like a heart.

"These look fabulous," he said, then popped it into his mouth.

Nancy saw a look of surprise cross Brock's

face, but all he said was "And they—uh—they taste fabulous, too!" He reached for another truffle, but Nancy noticed that he was wincing as he tried to chew it.

"I don't think he likes them," George commented, sounding puzzled.

Brock kept chewing. "I'll hate myself tomorrow," he said, "but—"

Abruptly he stopped. His face registered shock, not surprise any longer, Nancy noticed. Clutching his stomach, he moaned. "Sam, there's something wrong with these," he managed to get out.

There was a nervous titter from some of the guests.

"Oh, Brock, stop it," Samantha laughed. Giving him a jovial punch in the shoulder, she added, "He's such a kidder. Aren't you, Brock?"

Brock didn't answer. He just fell forward, bent over double.

Then, twisting in agony, he collapsed to the floor.

Chapter

Five

Nancy leapt to her feet and raced to him. "Brock, are you all right?" she asked urgently.

The only answer was a dreadful moan.

"Brock?" Samantha shouted in a panicked voice. *"Brock?"*

Bending over, Nancy shook his shoulder. At her touch Brock fell onto his back.

Bess screamed, and a chorus of gasps and cries rose from the other guests.

"What's the matter?" shouted a woman wearing a press pass. She rushed forward—but stopped short when she saw Brock. His face was gray and flecked with sweat, and his lips were drawn back into a shocking grimace of agony. His blue eyes were bulging and staring, as if he couldn't focus.

"Help me. Please!" he managed to gasp out.

"Is there a doctor here?" someone called.

"I'll call an ambulance," Jake Tagley spoke up in a take-charge tone. He dashed out the door.

"Brock, can you hear me?" Nancy asked as calmly as she could. "We're getting help."

Brock didn't respond. Nancy checked his pulse. It was shallow, and his wrist was icy.

Sobbing, Samantha threw herself down next to Brock. "Say something, Brock," she begged. "I can't believe this is happening!"

Gripping both of his hands tightly, she stared up at Nancy. "He's—he's not going to die, is he?"

But Nancy couldn't answer.

Half an hour later an ambulance pulled away from Oakwood Inn, carrying Brock to the hospital. Samantha had gone with him, so Mrs. Tagley was now frantically trying to put together an activity for the horrified guests.

Nancy, Bess, and George were still in the living room. A police car had arrived, and a gangling young officer named Steve Ullman was taking statements from the guests.

"You know, Nancy's a detective. She's incredible," Bess said proudly when it was her turn to be questioned. "You should let her work with you on this case."

Officer Ullman smiled politely. "We don't know if it's a case yet," he said, flipping to a new page of his notebook. "But, of course, I'd be grateful for any help any of you can give me."

"You should know about a couple of strange

things that happened earlier." Nancy told him about the "accidents" that had taken place that day and about her suspicion that Brock was poisoned. "His attack came right after he'd eaten the first piece of chocolate."

"Seems hard to believe it could work so fast without killing him," Officer Ullman mused. He was eyeing Nancy with more respect now. "I'm not a poison expert, but I'll definitely take those chocolates back to the lab. You say you found the jar of ants hidden in the kitchen? Do you think any of the kitchen staff could be responsible?"

"It's hard to think of a motive, but I can check it out for you," Nancy replied.

"I may be back myself, depending on what the lab boys turn up," said Officer Ullman. "In the meantime, let me know if you find anything."

Unfortunately, most of the staff had left for the evening by the time Nancy and her friends reached the kitchen. The lone waitress putting away some leftover chocolate-raspberry mousse torte had nothing to add to what the girls had seen for themselves.

"We'll have to try again tomorrow," Nancy said, pushing through the kitchen doors into the deserted dining room. "Let's go up to the suite. I'd like to go over what we know so far"—she frowned—"which isn't much."

"Oh, let's not go back up yet," said George. "Couldn't we find some other room where we could talk in private? Our suite's so small it makes me feel claustrophobic."

"Fine with me," said Nancy. "But nothing on

the first floor where anyone could interrupt us or listen in."

They settled on a small lounge in the basement that smelled as if it was a smoking room, probably for the staff.

"Well, Nan," George said, settling into a battered armchair. "It looks as though you have another case on your hands."

Nancy and Bess sat down on a couch covered with an Indian-print spread. "Whoever put the ants on that cake and tampered with the chocolate scale may have been playing a prank. But poisoning's no joke. Someone's definitely out to get Brock."

"But who would want to hurt him?" Bess asked. "I mean, an actor might have enemies, but you'd expect them to be—oh, I don't know, rivals for acting parts or something. Who would try to attack an actor at a chocolate festival?"

Three names popped into Nancy's head immediately. "Tim might," she said. "He's obviously jealous of Brock. And, maybe, Mrs. Tagley. She made the chocolates, so she had a perfect opportunity to poison them. I'm not sure what her motive would be, but I get the feeling that she's not crazy about Brock. I also don't trust Dan Avery. I have no idea what he's up to, but I did overhear him say he'd get Brock. Other than those three, I—"

Thwack! Thwack!

"What's that?" Bess asked. Nancy was the first to get up and walk to the doorway and out into the hall. A light was on in an adjoining room. A pool table stood in the middle of the room, and board games were scattered on card tables with fold-out chairs around them. On the far wall was a dart board, at which Jake Tagley was just aiming his third dart.

"It's Jake," she called back to Bess and George, who were still in the hall.

"Hi," Jake said to the girls as they came over to join him. "I couldn't think of anything else to do. This is supposed to relax me, but I'm not sure it'll work." Nancy noticed that Jake was speaking mostly to Bess.

"I don't blame you," Bess said sympathetically. "We feel terrible about Brock, too. What a nightmare!" She shivered, and Jake stepped closer as if to protect her. "It's just so spooky thinking that there's someone out there who could . . ." Bess's voice trailed off, and she shuddered again.

"Don't worry," said Jake, putting a hand on her shoulder. "I'll watch out for you."

He tried to sound as if he was half joking, but his admiring gaze made Nancy sure he meant what he said. From the glazed expression in Bess's blue eyes, however, Nancy realized that Jake's concern for her friend wasn't even registering.

Jake seemed to notice Bess's indifference as well. To change course, he checked his watch and sighed. "So much for my dart game. I guess I should go help my dad a little before I call it a night. He's a night owl and loves to work late. He's nailing down baseboards in the east wing."

"And we might as well head up to the lobby and see what's going on," Nancy said. "Maybe Mrs. Tagley has some news about Brock."

They found Samantha's mother sitting at the front desk going over some flow charts. Seeing the girls, she put down her pen wearily. "Were you looking for something to do?" she asked the girls. "I'm afraid our evening plans have fizzled out."

"We just wondered if there was any news about Brock," Bess said.

"He's not doing well at all."

Nancy thought she detected a strange note of satisfaction in Mrs. Tagley's voice. But why? Could it be that she disliked Brock so much that she was actually happy he was sick?

"Samantha called a little while ago," Mrs. Tagley went on. "Brock's in intensive care, unconscious. The doctors suggested that Samantha come home because there's nothing she can do for him right now."

Just then Nancy heard the front door open. She turned to see Samantha walking wearily up to the front desk, her face chalk white.

"M-Mother?"

"Hello, dear," said Mrs. Tagley worriedly. "How are you doing?"

Before Samantha could answer, Bess spoke up. "How's Brock doing?"

"No change from the last time I checked in.

But I can tell that the police think"—Samantha's dark eyes filled with tears—"that they feel Brock was poisoned," she choked out. "They were asking all kinds of questions about the chocolates. And about the guests here. And—and about Tim."

"What about Tim?" Mrs. Tagley asked quickly.

"Things like where he was when Brock got sick," Samantha said miserably, tears falling down her pale cheeks. "And whether he had access to the scale that dumped Brock into the chocolate. And if he had any reason to be jealous of Brock. Mother, I know they suspect Tim of poisoning Brock!"

"Oh, that's ridiculous," said Mrs. Tagley, but Nancy didn't think she sounded convinced.

"B-but if it wasn't Tim, then who was it?"

There was an awful silence.

"I can't believe this is happening," Samantha finally said, wiping her tears away. "I couldn't even face Tim right now. Things are awkward enough between us." Brushing back a wayward strand of long hair, she glanced at the grandfather clock by the front door. "I should go up to bed, but first I need a glass of milk."

"We should head upstairs, too," said Nancy to Bess and George. "I'm sure we've got a big day ahead of us." And not just tasting chocolate, she added wearily to herself.

Once they were in the elevator and out of earshot, Bess muttered, "I don't blame Tim for being upset. Samantha's just running away from her problems. I mean, why is she so cozy with Brock if she's going with someone else?"

"Maybe she's just confused and needs some time to work out her feelings," Nancy suggested.

George nudged Bess teasingly. "Come on. Admit it. Aren't you really just jealous that Sam is stringing two guys along?"

"No way," Bess said defensively. Then, giggling, she admitted, "Maybe just a little."

Five minutes later Bess was already in her nightgown, flipping through a magazine in the living room of the girls' suite.

"I'm too wide awake even to think about getting ready for bed," Nancy said. "George, want to help me search the downstairs living room one more time?"

"Sure. We'll let Bess get her beauty sleep." There was a mischievous twinkle in her brown eyes as she added, "She needs it after tiring herself out eating all that chocolate today."

The pillow Bess hurled just missed them as they slipped out the door.

Downstairs only a couple of lights were burning. Most of the rooms were shrouded in shadow, and there were no guests anywhere.

"Will you keep out of this?" an angry voice ripped through the darkness, causing Nancy and George to jump. The voice was rising high and shrill, and Nancy realized it was coming from behind the door to a lighted office. "You're not my father, you know!"

"I'm not trying to be your father!" It was Mr. Tagley's voice, and he sounded just as angry as Samantha. "I'm just suggesting that we bring someone in to give you a hand running this place until the festival is over! That doesn't seem like much, considering the strain you're under. The strain you're putting us *all* under."

"I'm not under any strain!" Samantha insisted in a tone that contradicted her words. "Stop trying to take the festival away from me!"

"Sam, maybe there *is* too much for one person to do—at the moment, anyway." This voice was Jake's, and he sounded much calmer than the other two. "Why don't you let me help you out? Dad can handle the construction in the east wing by himself, and I could give you a hand with the day-to-day stuff."

"No. *No,*" repeated Samantha in a cracked voice. "I'll do fine with the day-to-day stuff if you guys will just get off my back!"

"Well, you didn't exactly do a great job with those guests in Room two fourteen," Samantha's mother put in tartly. "If I hadn't been on hand to persuade them to stay, they would be long gone. And if you don't watch out, you're going to lose *all* the guests. People don't like wondering whether they're about to be poisoned, you know."

"It's not my fault they got the creeps!" Samantha shot back. "And how can you talk about losing guests? This inn was losing guests *and* money before you let me take over!"

"The only thing the guests care about are my desserts," her mother retorted. "My chocolate concoctions are the only reason people have come to this festival."

"Now, wait a minute, guys," Jake said mildly. "Why don't we all try to—"

Samantha wouldn't let him finish. "Oh, so *you're* the reason this festival got started, Mother?" she asked sarcastically. "I had nothing to do with it—is that what you're saying? After all, I *only* came up with the whole idea and handled all the publicity and convinced Brock to come and—"

"Brock Sawyer has brought us nothing but problems so far," Mrs. Tagley snapped. "He was your first mistake."

"You're all against me!" Samantha yelled. She sounded beside herself.

In the darkened hallway Nancy and George exchanged an uncomfortable glance. Nancy had been so shocked by all they were hearing that she hadn't even realized they were eavesdropping. With a tilt of her head Nancy suggested that they should start back to the lobby.

"No one's against you, Sam," came Mr. Tagley's faint voice. "Can't you see we're on your side? It's just that you can't be expected to work as hard as you have been."

"Oh, so you think I can't handle the work?" Even from down the hall, Samantha's voice was louder and shriller than before. Then Nancy heard the sound of a door being yanked open.

"I don't want to hear any more!" Samantha shouted. "You all *deserve* to have this festival fall apart!"

Chapter

Six

S HE'S COMING THIS WAY! Quick, get back!" Nancy whispered. She swiftly pulled George into a shadowed doorway.

Samantha swept by without appearing to notice the girls at all. Then she was gone.

There was nothing but silence coming from the office she had just left. Finally Nancy heard the sound of a chair scraping on the floor, as if someone was standing up. "Let's get back upstairs before the rest of them come out," she whispered to George. They tiptoed the few steps to the elevator, and Nancy punched the button. Thankfully, the doors slid open quickly, and Nancy and George ducked inside.

"This is even more of a soap opera than I thought," George commented.

Bess was still reading her magazine when Nancy and George got back to the suite.

"Wow!" she exclaimed softly after hearing what had happened. "I didn't realize that Samantha and her mother were *that* mad at each other. You don't think this festival is making Samantha a little crazy, do you?"

Nancy had been wondering about that herself. "She seemed ready to come unhinged tonight," she answered soberly as she sat down on the couch next to Bess.

"Unhinged enough to poison Brock, though?" George called from her little bedroom. She emerged a moment later in an oversize red T-shirt and plopped down in the worn armchair.

"I'm not sure," Nancy began thoughtfully, propping her long legs up on the coffee table. "She asked me not to investigate this case after I found that ant jar. I guess she *might* be trying to sabotage the festival herself—both to take the pressure off herself and to teach her family a lesson. Except that everything that's happened so far has been aimed at Brock, not the festival in general. Can you see Samantha trying to hurt Brock in that way?"

Both Bess and George shook their heads. "I can't see *anyone* trying to hurt him," Bess put in emphatically. "Poor Brock! I called the hospital while you were downstairs. They said he's in stable condition. I'm glad he's okay, but I'm *sick* from worrying about him."

"I notice you polished off the rest of that candy while Nancy and I were downstairs," George pointed out, grinning. "Maybe that's what's making you feel sick. Anyway, what about Jake Tagley? Did you forget about him?"

"Forget about Jake? What do you mean?" Bess sounded puzzled.

George's brown eyes were twinkling. "Well, Bess, you've certainly had a busy day. Jake's got a major crush on you, and you're so in love with Brock you haven't noticed!"

"I'm not in love with Brock *or* Jake," Bess said stiffly. "Besides, it's mean of you to joke about Brock when he's in the hospital."

"Brock's in good hands," Nancy reassured her. She got up from the couch and stretched. "Anyway, you guys should get some rest. Tomorrow's going to be busy."

"What about you?" asked George. "Aren't you going to bed?"

"Not yet. We were interrupted before we got to check out the living room, remember? I won't be able to fall asleep if I don't do it."

Bess's blue eyes opened wide. "But, Nan, you can't go down there alone. It's so late! Can't it wait until tomorrow morning?"

"Too risky," Nancy told her. "I don't want the cleaning staff to get the chance to clean the place up. They probably start early. I've got to check the room for clues tonight."

"Do you want me to come?" George asked.

"No, you're all ready for bed. I'll just hurry down and be right back up." After saying good night, Nancy stepped quietly out into the hall and moved toward the elevator.

Now every creak the elevator made seemed loud enough to wake the whole inn. Nancy held her breath when the door clanged open in the lobby—but the first floor was dark and deserted. No one was there to see her tiptoe across the lobby and into the living room.

Did she dare switch on a light? It was so dark that Nancy knew she had no choice. Feeling along the wall inside the doorway, she clicked on the light switch, blinking in the sudden brightness.

As she made her way across the room, she saw that the end tables were littered with glasses, crumpled napkins, festival schedules, and ashtrays. There was a faint trail on the Oriental carpet of what appeared to be sawdust footprints leading from the fireplace to a side door.

Sawdust? Nancy suddenly asked herself. What was sawdust doing in the living room? There wasn't any construction there!

She gently pushed open the side door. The tracks led into a narrow hallway that Nancy hadn't been down before. Leaving the side door ajar so she could see by the light from the living room, she stepped out and followed the yellow footprints to—

"The kitchen," Nancy murmured aloud. "Another entrance to the kitchen!"

She held her breath as she switched on a kitchen light—then let out a huge sigh of disappointment.

The trail of sawdust ended right at the kitchen door. The busboy Nancy had spoken to earlier obviously hadn't been exaggerating when he described how clean the kitchen was kept. The floor was gleaming brightly enough to be used in a floor wax commercial!

Then Nancy's gaze landed on something else. On the counter right next to the light switch, within easy reach of the door, was a huge pile of Silk and Cream chocolate boxes. They were stacked in neat rows against the wall. Nancy noted that the stack closest to the door had one less box than the others. She was willing to bet that it had been the box that poisoned Brock.

Had the poisoner gotten into the kitchen to alter the chocolates before Samantha brought them out? Was the sawdust a clue? If it was, whoever had tracked it in had probably come from the east wing of the inn. That pointed to someone who had been working there—probably Jake, Tim, or Mr. Tagley. A visitor to the east wing might have picked up a little sawdust on his or her shoes, but not enough to leave an actual trail.

"Hmmm," Nancy murmured aloud. It wasn't much of a clue—more of a hint really.

Just then her mouth stretched open in an enormous yawn. You've done enough for one day, Drew. The case will have to wait until morning. Yawning again, she tiptoed back toward the elevator.

"I think I'm going to skip the brownie workshop," Nancy told Bess and George the following morning after breakfast. "I want to head over to the police lab. They may have figured out what poisoned Brock by now."

"Do you want us to come?" Bess asked reluctantly, twisting her blond hair in her fingers. "I'd hate to miss trying the ultimate brownie, but—"

"Go on," said Nancy, laughing. "I'll be fine. The workshop sounds like a lot of fun."

George groaned and tugged at the waist of her jeans. "After those chocolate-chip pancakes we just had, I may never eat again. It seems kind of soon to be making brownies."

"Speak for yourself!" Bess sounded shocked.

The police station and lab was about a half-hour's drive from the Oakwood Inn. The technician on duty in the lab, a woman in her thirties named Officer Sherbinski, greeted Nancy coolly but politely.

"Officer Ullman told me you were coming," she said. "He said it was fine to answer any questions you might have." She directed Nancy to a small table, and they sat down.

"Any word on how Brock's doing?"

"Mr. Sawyer is conscious, but he's feeling too weak to talk," Officer Sherbinski replied. "A detective went to the hospital to question him, but he wasn't up to it."

"I see," said Nancy. "Do you know yet what kind of poison was used?"

Officer Sherbinski nodded. "Yes. Mercurous chloride. Its common name is calomel."

"Calomel? I don't think I've heard of it."

"It's a white, tasteless powder that was once

used as a purgative. People took it to clean out their systems," the officer explained. "It's not used much nowadays. It can do a lot of damage —especially to the liver and kidneys. Mr. Sawyer is lucky to be alive."

"He certainly is," Nancy agreed. "Were all the chocolates in the box poisoned?"

Giving Nancy a meaningful look, the officer said, "Well, that's where it gets complicated. There wasn't any mercurous chloride in the chocolates. None at all. They were clean."

"What?" Nancy said, leaning forward over the table. She didn't suppose there was any way the poisoner could have tainted only the chocolates Brock ate, since there couldn't be any way of knowing which ones they'd be. "That means you have no idea how Brock was poisoned," she said at last.

"Exactly. According to the report"—Officer Sherbinski tapped a manila folder resting on the table—"dinner was served buffet-style. There's no way the culprit could have singled out Brock's food."

Nancy sighed. "We're totally in the dark then."

Nancy stepped out of her car and walked slowly across the parking lot toward the inn, her shoes crunching on the gravel. She wasn't sure how to proceed with the case. At least Brock was safe in the hospital for the time being. But with him out of the picture, the culprit would probably lie low. Nancy would have to work with the few clues that she already had.

Deep in thought, Nancy pushed open the door and stepped into the lobby. The scene there brought her sharply back to the present.

A tearful Samantha was standing by the front desk, her arms around Tim Krueger. Next to her were two police officers—Officer Ullman and another young man. A cluster of guests had gathered, too. From their expressions, Nancy guessed the officers weren't there to join in the Chocolate Festival.

"You can't take him away!" Samantha was sobbing. "I won't let you!"

Jolted into action, Nancy stepped forward to join Samantha. "What's going on?" she asked.

"Nothing for you to be concerned about, Miss Drew," Officer Ullman told her calmly. "We're just taking Mr. Kreuger in for questioning."

"Questioning?" Nancy repeated.

"That's right. He's our main suspect in the attempted murder of Brock Sawyer."

Chapter

Seven

SEEING NANCY, Samantha turned to her.

"Nancy, I know Tim didn't do it. You've got to find out what really happened," she begged. Tears were streaming down her cheeks. "I don't have anyone else to turn to!"

Samantha let out a little moan as the police led Tim toward the door. She, Nancy, Bess, and George followed them outside and stood watching as the police car sped away with Tim inside.

"I'll be happy to take on the case," Nancy told Samantha quietly. She didn't mention that she'd already begun investigating. "Should we talk in your office?"

"I guess that would be better than broadcasting *all* my problems to the guests," Samantha said with a wan smile. "They know more than enough already."

Straightening up with determination, she led the way through the lobby and down the hall to her office. Samantha sat at her desk, motioning the girls toward chairs.

"The whole inn must know Tim was arrested," Samantha groaned.

"Maybe that's best right now," Nancy suggested. "If your guests think the problem's been taken care of, they might start to relax again. And if the real culprit is someone else—and if he or she thinks that Tim is the only suspect—then that person might start getting careless."

"So you don't suspect Tim?" Samantha asked, brightening. "Oh, I'm so glad!"

"Well, I certainly don't think the case against him is airtight," Nancy replied carefully. "It's the fight Tim picked with Brock that makes him the most likely suspect to the police. But picking a fight with someone is a long way from poisoning him."

"That's right," George put in hopefully.

"I *know* Tim didn't poison Brock," Samantha said firmly. "He—he certainly had a motive. But I've known Tim for a long time. There's no way he'd be so vicious."

"I hope you're right," said Nancy. "And if he didn't, then we need to find out if anyone else has a bone to pick with Brock Sawyer." She got to her feet. "Why don't you go back to your guests now, Samantha, while we get to work. The minute we turn something up, we'll let you know."

A sheepish expression came over Samantha's

face as she asked, "How would you feel about keeping me company for lunch? I don't feel as if I can face eating in the dining room with all those people around." She plucked nervously at one of the combs in her hair. "I've got a few phone calls to make, but then would you like to grab a sandwich in here with me?"

"Sounds great," said Nancy. They agreed to meet in forty-five minutes.

"I didn't want to say this in front of Samantha," Nancy told her friends when they were out in the lobby, "but we definitely can't rule Tim out. There's no way I can question him when he's in police custody, though. Let's start our questioning with Dan Avery, since I did hear him make a threat about getting some actor. It's about time we found out what he was talking about. George, you want to come along?"

"What about me? Should I question Brock?" Bess asked hopefully.

"Not quite," Nancy told her, smiling. "You can do the next best thing and spend time getting to know Jake Tagley better."

Bess's blue eyes widened. "You think Jake's a suspect? What could he have against Brock?"

"I have no idea," said Nancy, "but he may be able to shed some light on what the people around the inn think of Brock. Just turn on the charm, Bess, and see what you come up with."

"You've got it!" Bess said brightly. Then, gesturing to her stained T-shirt and shorts, she added, "But first I'd better change. I can't get to know Jake in clothes that are covered with brownie batter!"

Nancy and George knocked on Dan Avery's door, but there was no answer. He wasn't in the basement playing Chocolate Trivia or taking a chocolate pastry class with Mrs. Tagley or participating in an auction of chocolate-related cooking supplies. In fact, he was nowhere to be found.

"Okay, on to plan B," Nancy said, running a hand through her hair. "Let's try some members of the staff instead. The waiters who work in the dining room might have something to tell us."

Most of the waiting staff were too busy setting up for lunch to talk to Nancy and George, but two waitresses named Karen and Liz agreed to spare the girls a few minutes. After a brief explanation of her involvement in the case, Nancy asked, "Has either of you noticed anything in the kitchen that seems out of the ordinary? Even the smallest discrepancy could be a clue."

The two waitresses considered the question. "Well, Mrs. Tagley's been in the kitchen more than usual," said Liz slowly. She had a round face and curly dark hair. "It's not exactly unusual, since so many of her desserts are being prepared for the festival. But it seems as though she's in there constantly."

"Is she cooking or just checking up on things?" asked Nancy.

"She's definitely not cooking," said Karen immediately. "Mrs. Tagley hates to cook where people can watch her. Says she can't concentrate if she feels like people are looking over her shoulder. She usually makes everything in the family's private kitchen upstairs—you know, where her apartment is. Then she has the stuff brought down to the main kitchen."

Nancy was intrigued by this detail. She didn't know what Mrs. Tagley's motive might be. But Samantha's mother certainly had the perfect opportunity to poison anything she made. "But what was she doing in the kitchen if she wasn't cooking?"

Both waitresses shrugged. "Beats me," said Karen. "Maybe it makes her feel more in control." She stared uneasily over her shoulder. "Uh, we should really go back to work."

Nancy thanked the waitresses for their time, then she and George headed back to Samantha's office.

"It's nice of you to keep me company," Samantha said gratefully when they arrived. "All those guests staring at me is a little hard to take." She reached for the telephone on her desk. "Let me just give a quick call down to room service and order us something."

"You have room service here?" asked George.

"You can just get sandwiches, coffee, things like that."

"Sounds good to me," said Nancy cheerfully. The girls chatted until their order arrived, and then Nancy said, "I've been wanting to learn a little more about your background, Samantha. When did you meet Brock?"

Samantha took a sip of iced tea. "Let me see,

the summer after my freshman year. Brock was in summer stock here." She smiled, remembering. "He was the lead in *Brigadoon*. It's kind of hard to imagine when you see him playing a cop on TV, but he was great."

She took a bite of her turkey sandwich before continuing. "Oakwood's got a pretty good summer stock company, considering we're way out in the sticks like this. Actually, Brock grew up in an even tinier town than Oakwood, about thirty miles from here. I used to wonder if that was why my mother disapproved of him so much. Maybe she didn't want me hanging around with someone who was from an even smaller town than I was."

"Your mother disapproved of Brock?" Nancy asked, glancing up alertly. "I didn't realize that."

Samantha grimaced. "She practically bit my head off when I first mentioned his name. You can't believe how hard she made my life the whole time I was going out with him." She shook her head. "Mothers. I swear, there's no way to keep them happy."

George had been munching on her roast beef sandwich while she listened. Now she asked, "But your mother doesn't dislike Brock anymore, does she?"

"No. She wasn't crazy about having him come for the festival, but at least she didn't throw a fit about it. I mean, it's good publicity for the inn and for her new line of chocolates. Or it was. They're certainly getting bad publicity now," Samantha added bitterly. Then she glanced at her watch. "I've really got to get back to work," she said regretfully. "We're setting up a chocolate fondue demonstration, and I have to go track down some chairs. Thanks for keeping me company."

The three girls left the office at the same time, but Nancy was careful to head in the opposite direction from Samantha. "Hmm," she said to George when they were far enough away. "So Mrs. Tagley doesn't like Brock. It fits, in a way. She seemed happy when he was talking about leaving. Now I just have to find out why."

"Why don't you ask her?" suggested George.

"Good idea," said Nancy. "She's going to be giving chocolate classes all afternoon, though—I checked the schedule. So let's talk to some of the employees first. I remember Jake saying that some of them have been here even longer than Mrs. Tagley has."

"I can't discuss my boss," the gray-haired gardener explained gruffly. "That would be unprofessional."

As the older man turned back to clipping the azalea bushes by the front entrance, Nancy looked at George and shrugged.

"That's the fourth person we've tried," George said as they stepped out of the heat and back into the cool lobby. "It doesn't seem like any of the old-timers want to talk to us."

Nancy tucked her hands into the pockets of her shorts. "That's for sure. 'In a close-knit place like this,'" Nancy went on, mimicking the gravelly voice of one of the older chefs, " 'you never know what's going to get back to people.' "

George laughed at Nancy's imitation. Nancy sighed and said, "I'm starting to think we've wasted the whole afternoon."

"What about trying the person in charge of room service, or whatever they call it here?" George suggested. "We haven't been there yet."

"Good idea." Nancy smiled as she added, "You know, I think this will be the first time I've ever seen anyone who works in room service. I've always just thought of those people as voices on the phone before."

The woman they met in the small basement service kitchen was a lot more than a voice on the phone. She was a wiry woman named Mrs. Reames, with curly gray hair and glasses. She seemed to be in her seventies and was very happy to get the chance to talk—a lot—to Nancy and George.

"I spend all day listening to people order hamburgers," she said, once Nancy explained why they were there. "It would be a pleasure to get to talk for once. I've seen this place go through a lot of changes. Oh, they've tried to retire me a couple of times, but I tell them I'm not leaving until they drag me out. So what if I get the orders mixed up once in a while? It's not as if—"

"I bet you have some fascinating stories to tell about the old days," Nancy said quickly. She hated to interrupt, but she didn't want to spend all afternoon listening to stories about mixed-up orders. "You must have been here for nearly as long as Mrs. Tagley—is that right?"

"Longer! I was here before she and her first husband ever bought the place. 'Course, Mrs. Patton—I mean Mrs. Tagley—was the real power behind the throne, you might say. Samantha's father never did have the gumption she did. But then, I guess that's why they moved out to the country in the first place."

"Because Mr. Patton didn't—didn't have enough gumption?" George asked, leaning against the counter.

"Well, because his business had failed, I mean," clarified Mrs. Reames. "He'd had some kind of nervous collapse after that businessman got through with him, and he and the missus bought the inn to give him more quiet surroundings. Ha! More quiet, my foot! Why, I can remember—"

"You said 'after that businessman got through with him,'" Nancy gently reminded Mrs. Reames. "Who do you mean?"

"Why, he was—he was—the name escapes me now," said Mrs. Reames. The room service telephone rang just then, but she ignored it. "Let them wait! They won't starve! Well, whatever his name was, it was a real scandal, what he did to Mr. Patton. Said he was going into partnership with him. Got him to sign a lot of bad checks—and just cleaned him out. Mr. Patton never could hold his head up after that—"

Mrs. Reames snapped her fingers so suddenly

that her glasses nearly fell off the end of her nose. "Sawyer! That was it, Mr. Sawyer!"

Nancy just stared at Mrs. Reames for a moment before asking, "Mr. Sawyer? Any relation to Brock Sawyer?"

"That actor? Yup. That's the one. He's sitting pretty high in the saddle now, isn't he? But his background is nothing to be proud of. I'm not surprised Mrs. Patton—I mean Mrs. Tagley— can't stand the sight of him." Mrs. Reames shot Nancy and George a knowing look.

"After all, the boy's own father as good as murdered her husband."

Chapter

Eight

SUDDENLY Mrs. Reames's face froze. "You won't tell Mrs. Tagley I've been blabbing on about her like this, will you?" she begged, twisting her apron. "I'd probably get in all kinds of trouble!"

"I promise we'll keep your secret," Nancy told her. She stood up to leave. "Thank you so much. Come on, George."

"You were right, George," said Nancy as she and George took the stairs up to the main floor. "This really *is* a soap opera!"

George asked, "Do you think Mrs. Tagley could have been trying to get revenge on Brock for what his father did to her first husband?"

"It's possible," said Nancy. "I hope not, though. I like Samantha. It would be terrible for her if her mother had done something like that.

72

And that reminds me of something else. Does Samantha know about the way Brock's father treated *her* father? I mean, does she know she fell in love with the son of the man who destroyed her father's spirit?"

George shrugged. "I guess that's one of the things you can find out when you talk to Mrs. Tagley. You are going to talk to her, aren't you?"

"You bet—very, very carefully. I really don't want to get Mrs. Reames in trouble, so I'll have to tiptoe around the whole thing. Let's see, what time is it?" Nancy checked her watch. "Four-thirty. I don't think there are any more activities scheduled for this afternoon. This is probably as good a time as any to talk to Mrs. Tagley."

"Want me to come?" asked George. "Or do you think she might say more if I'm not around?"

"I guess I should try a personal approach," said Nancy. "Maybe you can track down Bess and Jake."

"Will do. Good luck!" George headed for the elevator.

Nancy found Mrs. Tagley's office next to Samantha's—the door open. When Nancy peeked in, she saw that Samantha's mother was talking on the telephone.

"You'll be done working by dinnertime, won't you?" she snapped into the receiver. There was a short pause, then she said, "Well, what about my dessert demonstration tonight? It would be nice to see you once in a while, instead of having you work every second." She paused again, then sighed. "Oh. Well, okay. Listen, put on a tie if you get a chance, won't you?"

She hung up. Seeing Nancy, Mrs. Tagley smiled ruefully and said, "I'm married to a workaholic. He'd rather finish a staircase than eat. Can you imagine?"

Nancy wasn't sure what to say, but fortunately Mrs. Tagley didn't wait for her to answer. "Well, I'm sure you didn't come to listen to me complain about my husband. Have a seat, Nancy. My daughter's told me you're looking into Brock's poisoning. Is that what you've come to talk to me about?"

"That's right," Nancy said, sitting down. "I'm trying to find out who might have had a motive."

"I should have thought that was easy," said Mrs. Tagley. Was there a wary look in her eyes now? Nancy wondered. "Poor Tim has a pretty good reason."

"He does," Nancy agreed, "but so do some other people." She took a deep breath before asking, "How did you feel about Brock?"

Now Mrs. Tagley was definitely on the alert. "How *did* I feel?" she repeated, staring at Nancy. "You sound as if he's dead or something. I like him fine."

"Samantha told me that you objected when she first started dating Brock." That, at least, wouldn't get Mrs. Reames into trouble.

"Well, they did get serious awfully fast." Mrs. Tagley gave an uneasy laugh. "Besides, I have to admit I have an old-fashioned prejudice against actors. You never know if they're suddenly going to be out of work."

"That's hardly a problem for Brock now."

"No. It's not." Mrs. Tagley fell silent.

"I've heard a rumor," Nancy said carefully, "that Brock's father and your first husband had a falling-out."

In an instant all pretense of cordiality vanished from Mrs. Tagley's face. "Where did you hear that?"

"It seems to be common knowledge." Nancy knew she was stretching the truth a little—but surely more of the staff than Mrs. Reames knew about Brock's father. "I don't mean to pry, Mrs. Tagley, but I'm sure you can see that this information has a bearing on the case."

For a long moment Mrs. Tagley merely stared at Nancy. Then, letting out a long breath, she said, "My first husband, Lloyd Patton, was a very successful realtor. He was a brilliant businessman, but he was also very temperamental—you could almost say unstable."

Samantha seemed to have inherited some of his temperament, Nancy thought.

Mrs. Tagley's eyes focused far off as she explained. "As long as things were going right for him, he got through his days all right. But whenever he was disappointed or worried about something, he seemed to feel it ten times more than the average person.

"So along came Brock's father—who was also named Brock, by the way." Mrs. Tagley's eyes flicked to Nancy. "I bet you thought Brock's name was made up, didn't you?"

"I did, now that you mention it," Nancy admitted with a smile. "It's so perfect for TV."

"Anyway, Brock Sawyer senior had all the charm of his son and then some. He told Lloyd he had a great idea for doubling their incomes. They would go into partnership to develop a retirement community in Arizona. Lloyd would put up the capital while Brock senior handled the actual developing. He told Lloyd he didn't want to bother him with the day-to-day stuff."

Mrs. Tagley shuddered at the memory. "Well, my husband loved the idea. He found investors. He found potential buyers. He put everything he had into that business—his assets *and* his good name. And—well, I guess you know what happened next."

"Mr. Sawyer didn't hold up his end of the bargain," Nancy said quietly.

"Hah! That's a mild way of putting it!" Nancy thought Mrs. Tagley was about to launch into an angry tirade, but she just took a deep breath, as if to calm herself. She continued, "Lloyd lost all his money—and his investors' money. He never forgave himself for that. He was never a happy man again. Brock Sawyer destroyed him."

Nancy felt terrible about bringing up such painful memories, but she knew it was the only way to get at the truth of Brock's poisoning. "That's when you moved out here to the inn?" she asked.

Mrs. Tagley nodded. "We thought we could

make a go of it—that it would be a pleasant and maybe relaxing way to support ourselves. Shows how much we knew about innkeeping," she said with a snort. "I liked our new life, but Lloyd just couldn't make the adjustment. His health started failing after a couple of months, and he went downhill very fast.

"The doctor said it was heart failure. I'd call it heartbreak. My husband died of grief." Tears suddenly sprang to Mrs. Tagley's eyes. "So now you know."

Nancy still had one more question. "But Samantha doesn't, does she?" she asked gently.

"No. I've kept all this from her. I hope you will, too." Mrs. Tagley leaned forward, gripping the edge of her desk intently. "But whatever problems I had with Brock Sawyer senior are in the past. All of this really has no bearing on what's happened to his son."

Unless Mrs. Tagley had poisoned Brock, of course.

"And that was pretty much all she'd say," Nancy told Bess and George as they were sipping glasses of iced tea in the living room. The spacious room was once again immaculate, and the girls were sitting on a window seat in a bay window that overlooked the inn's front lawn and flower beds. "If she is the one who poisoned Brock, it'll be hard to prove it."

"I feel sorry for her," said George. "I thought she was just kind of stern, but now I can see why."

"I can, too," Nancy said, "not that being sorry for her means she's not a suspect." Turning to Bess, Nancy asked, "Did Jake tell you anything that might be useful?"

"Not exactly," said Bess, her mouth curving into a hint of a smile. "He did mention that he couldn't figure out what was going on between Samantha and Brock. But I'm afraid we didn't get around to discussing the case much. . . ." Her voice trailed off, and a furious blush spread up her face.

Crossing her arms over her chest, Nancy asked, "Just what *did* you do?"

Bess grinned at the memory. "Well, Jake took me out for pizza for lunch—said he was getting sick of chocolate. Then we drove around the countryside and just talked. He's really a nice guy, Nancy! Funny, considerate—and he's a *great* listener."

George's expression indicated she was dubious. "Is he nicer than Brock?"

"Well, I don't really know Brock," said Bess with a dismissive wave. She made it sound as if she'd never even glanced in Brock's direction before. "Do you guys think we could extend our visit a little?" she went on in an excited rush.

Nancy sighed. "We may have to, if I don't come any closer to solving this case than I did today."

"Oh, give yourself a break," Bess told her. "You're doing a great job." Jumping up, she started in the direction of the elevator. "Let's go up and get dressed for dinner. Jake asked us to sit with them."

An hour later Nancy, Bess, and George entered the dining room and headed for the Tagleys' table. The girls had all changed into dresses, but Jake seemed to notice only Bess. Nancy had to admit Bess looked terrific in her flowered minidress. Jake wasn't bad himself, in his white pants, blue shirt, and navy blazer.

The girls said hello to Jake and Samantha. Mr. and Mrs. Tagley weren't around and Nancy wondered if Mrs. Tagley—like her daughter at lunch —hadn't been able to face eating in public after the emotional scene in her office.

"Don't tell me there's chocolate in *this!*" Nancy exclaimed as a waiter set a plate of chicken with dark, spicy-looking sauce in front of her a few minutes later.

"Well, there is," Samantha told her, laughing. "That's a mole sauce. It's a Mexican recipe that uses unsweetened chocolate. You can't really taste the chocolate, but it adds wonderfully to the flavor."

"It's delicious," said Nancy after she'd taken a bite. "I can't wait to tell Ned I ate *chicken* with chocolate!"

"Save some room for dessert," Samantha cautioned. "After my mom's cooking demonstration, we're going to pass around a big selection— all chocolate, of course."

"That sounds wonderful," said Nancy. "I'm in."

"Well, I hope you all have a great time," Samantha said.

Jake shot his sister a startled look. "You're not coming?"

"I can't. I'm going to visit Tim. I—I can't just forget about him while he's in police custody, can I?"

"Of course not," George said warmly.

"Make sure you notice Jake's handiwork, too. This will be the first time we're using the conference room in the east wing. He's done a great job restoring it."

The work showed, Nancy thought when she walked into the new conference room after dinner. The room was on the second floor, with windows running all along one side. The other three walls were papered in a woven fabric Nancy thought was cheerful and businesslike at the same time. The ceiling's acoustical tiles kept the room from echoing even though it was full of people. A big oval table was set up at one end of the long room. At the other end rows of chairs were lined up facing the new wooden stage. A demonstration table was set in the center of it. Jake was inside and directing people to sit.

Going over to him, Nancy said, "This room looks great, Jake. Did you and your father do all the work yourselves?"

"Yeah, but my dad was the real mastermind. I just held nails for him."

"I bet you did more than that," Bess piped up, moving up beside them. "Anyway, it's beautiful."

Jake nervously brushed his sandy hair back, as if embarrassed. But his hazel eyes were filled with pride. After finding the girls chairs at the end of one row, he continued seating the other guests.

Glancing around, Nancy saw that the room was already almost full, and a couple of photographers had stationed themselves near the stage. It seemed odd that Dan Avery wasn't among them, she thought, considering how he'd practically stomped all over everyone trying to get shots of some of the other events. Come to think of it, Nancy hadn't seen him all day. Where could he be?

Before she could wonder any further, Mrs. Tagley strode briskly onto the stage, and everyone started clapping. Then, with a quick bow, Mrs. Tagley announced, "Tonight I'll be preparing a dessert I call Chocolate Volcano. It's a spectacular finale to any meal, and it's a fun dessert to demonstrate because it's so dramatic. I'm going to need an audience volunteer. Who'd like to help me?"

A forest of hands popped into the air.

"How would *you* like to help?" she asked, pointing straight at Nancy.

"Me?" Nancy asked in surprise. She hadn't even had her hand up. "But I—"

"Go ahead. It'll be fun," whispered Bess eagerly.

"How can you resist?" George chimed in, grinning.

"Well, okay—why not?" Nancy stood up and began making her way toward the stage.

Bess was right. Working on the Chocolate Volcano *was* fun. Together Nancy and Mrs. Tagley shaped a mound of chocolate mousse into the shape of a mountain. Then Mrs. Tagley showed Nancy how to roll out a sheet of chocolate "leather"—made of chocolate mixed with corn syrup—and how to fit the leather neatly over the "mountain," leaving a hole at the top.

"Why do I suddenly feel all thumbs?" asked Nancy with a laugh. She happened to glance out at the audience as she spoke and saw that Jake had taken her chair and was whispering something in Bess's ear. Bess smiled at him, and then Jake slipped quietly out of the conference room.

"And now comes the most realistic touch," Mrs. Tagley was saying cheerfully. She seemed more relaxed than Nancy had ever seen her. Obviously, cooking and chocolate brought out the best in her. "I'm talking about the molten lava."

"Lava?" Nancy repeated in mock alarm. "Sounds dangerous!"

"Not at all. First we pour a half-cup of rum into the hole at the top of the mountain." Mrs. Tagley handed over the rum, and Nancy poured it in carefully.

"Next, we light the flame. The rum will begin to burn, and that's what makes the 'lava.' There won't be any alcohol left after it burns off, so you younger people will be able to sample this. Now to light the flame!" From a drawer under the table, Mrs. Tagley pulled out a miniature acetylene torch.

"Now, that *really* looks dangerous!" someone in the crowd called out.

There was a little nervous laughter before Mrs. Tagley said reassuringly, "It's not. Honestly, it's one of the most important cooking tools I own."

Mrs. Tagley pressed a button on the torch, and a thin spurt of blue flame leapt out. Carefully she aimed the flame at the rum that was now streaming down the sides of the cake. In an instant the rum was ablaze.

"There's your volcano!" she announced triumphantly—and the audience burst into spontaneous applause.

Just then Nancy was distracted by a thin cloud of white powder drifting down from the ceiling and settling in the air around her.

"Hey!" said Nancy, waving to try to clear the air. "Where did *that*—"

A muffled explosion cut off the rest of her sentence.

Before anyone had time to move, Nancy was surrounded by a sheet of flame!

Chapter

Nine

FOR THE REST of her life Nancy would be grateful that she'd so often rehearsed what to do in a fire emergency. Without conscious thought she dropped to the ground and rolled rapidly over and over until the flames licking at her clothes were out. Then, panting, she jumped to her feet. She had acted so swiftly that she hadn't been burned at all. One sleeve of her blouse was slightly charred, but that was the extent of the burns.

Checking Mrs. Tagley, Nancy saw that the woman, though white and shaking, was also unharmed. The fire had spread by then to the stage curtains behind them and the audience had panicked and was screaming and running for the exit.

"Where's a fire extinguisher?" Nancy called loudly to Mrs. Tagley, above the din.

Mrs. Tagley's mouth opened, but she didn't make a sound. She was swaying and gripping the edge of the table as though she were about to pass out.

Nancy peered out at the audience, frantically checking the room for a fire extinguisher. There had to be one— Yes! There it was, hanging on the wall next to a circuit breaker. She ran to it, yanked it from the wall, and raced back to the fire.

As she reached the stage, the curtain ripped from its metal frame and tumbled to the floor, a mass of flames that spread across the entire width of the platform.

Nancy yanked back the pin on the fire extinguisher and aimed it at the flames. Foam shot out, dousing the fire. In seconds the flames were out, and the curtain was a black, smoldering tangle on the floor.

Drawing a deep breath, Nancy checked on Mrs. Tagley again. She was still leaning against the table for support and was quite obviously in shock.

There were only a few people left in the conference room now, and one hysterical voice kept calling out over and over.

"Nancy! Nancy! Are you all right?"

It was Bess.

"I'm fine," Nancy called back shakily. "But I

don't feel like making another Chocolate Volcano for a long, long time."

"Now, explain to me just why you turned off the sprinkler system," the fire chief was saying patiently to Samantha.

"I knew that the dessert was going to be flambéed," Samantha said shakily. "I was afraid that the flames would set off the sprinkler, so—so I switched off the system. I'll never do it again," she added in a small voice.

The fire chief's expression softened. "Okay. I'm holding you to that."

Nancy was standing a little to the side with Bess and George, frowning. Something seemed wrong to her. She wasn't an expert, of course, but she was pretty sure flambéing a dessert wouldn't set off a sprinkler system. Was Samantha lying? Had she turned off the sprinkler in preparation for what was to come?

With a start, Nancy realized the fire chief was now talking to her. "You're a lucky girl. If you hadn't been so quick on your feet, that flour could have burned the whole room down in a matter of minutes."

"That powder was just flour?" said George incredulously. "I thought it was some kind of explosive."

"It was, in a way. Flour's just like any fine powder. It can be an explosive if the individual particles have lots of air around them," the chief explained. "All it takes is a spark and—well, you saw what happened."

Nancy shuddered. "I certainly did."

Turning back to Samantha, the fire chief said, "I know this was a cooking demonstration, but can you tell me one more thing? How did that flour happen to fall?"

"I don't know, Chief," Samantha said, shaking her head. "Maybe my mother does, but I—I don't think she should be disturbed tonight."

Samantha had missed the visiting hours to see Tim, so she had arrived back just after the fire department—or, at least, that was her claim. She had taken one look at her mother and called their family doctor, who had prescribed a sedative and sent Mrs. Tagley to bed.

"Well, I was just asking," said the chief, shrugging. "Probably there's a simple explanation."

But that wasn't what Nancy thought.

The Chocolate Volcano didn't contain any flour. Nancy had seen the recipe. And even if the dessert *had* needed flour, the flour would have been in a canister on the table—not drifting down from the ceiling.

One thing was for sure—once everything settled down and the conference room was empty again, Nancy was going to find out how flour got up to the ceiling.

It was another two hours before Nancy could go back to the room to investigate. She'd found a ladder in a nearby room and dragged it up onto the stage. She set it up and climbed up to get a close look at the ceiling.

Nancy's lips tightened. A small hole had been

drilled in the ceiling tile directly above the spot where the demonstration table had stood.

So her suspicions had been right! She saw that the tile could be lifted from its frame. She pushed it up carefully and peered into the gloomy crawlspace above the ceiling.

There, lying on its side on a beam, was a five-pound bag of flour.

Nancy tested the frame that the tiles were set into. It seemed to be strong enough to support a person's weight, but the beam definitely would be.

Someone had probably perched on the beam and poured flour through the hole. Someone who knew it would burst into flames in Nancy's face!

"It was Mrs. Tagley, Nancy," Bess said decisively, squeezing toothpaste onto her toothbrush. The three girls had crowded into the single bathroom and were going over the case as they washed up before bed. "It had to be. That fainting act of hers was just that—an act. She was out to stop you because you were getting too close to the truth about her poisoning Brock!"

"I don't know about that," said George. She finished splashing water on her face and reached past Bess for a towel. "If she was faking it, she's a pretty good actress. But we *do* know it couldn't have been Tim. He's still in police custody."

"You're right," Nancy said from her perch on the edge of the bathtub. "Whoever poured the flour down obviously wanted to stop my investigation. Mrs. Tagley's definitely my strongest suspect right now. I remember thinking it was odd that she picked me out of the crowd like that. Maybe she had the whole thing planned. Of course, she couldn't have poured the flour while she was standing right next to me. But she could have rigged the bag so that some of the flour would spill during the demonstration.

"I'm still wondering about Dan Avery, too," Nancy went on. "He wasn't around during the demonstration. He could have hidden above the ceiling and waited. I went down to the front desk and asked about him after checking out the conference room. The clerk said she hadn't seen him since yesterday. Have either of you?"

Bess and George shook their heads. "He's so gross I almost *hope* he's the culprit," said Bess.

"Actually, though," Nancy went on, "there's another person who wasn't at the demonstration tonight—Samantha. And if there's anyone who could have slipped into the conference room with a bag of flour, it's her. No one would question what she was doing."

Bess pulled her blond hair off her face with a terry headband and bent over the sink to wash her face. "Yes, but why would she want to attack you, Nancy?" she said, frowning. "Samantha wouldn't have done anything to hurt Brock, so she wouldn't have any reason to stop your investigation. Besides, she *asked* you to investigate this case—remember?"

Nancy nodded. "She doesn't seem to have any

kind of motive, either. All I'm saying is that she had the *opportunity* to rig the conference room. She turned off the sprinkler system, too."

"Wait—there's one other person who had the same opportunity as Sam *and* who wasn't at the demonstration tonight," said George slowly. She'd retreated to the doorway to give the others more room. "Not at it most of the time, anyway— Jake."

"*Jake!*" Bess gasped sharply. "George, you've got to be kidding! Jake wouldn't hurt a fly! Besides, he had a perfectly good reason for leaving the demonstration. He told me he had to finish varnishing a section of floor in the east wing."

"Hmm," said Nancy, considering. "Jake would have had plenty of chances to rig the conference room. But I can't think of any reason he'd want to poison Brock. So why would he want me out of the way? We certainly can't rule him out, but—"

"Yes, you can," Bess cut in, still obviously distressed. "Rule him out right now."

"Actually, I think that what I should do now— what we *all* should do—is get some sleep," said Nancy.

"Good idea," George agreed. "But I hope I don't dream about chocolate waffles—or what-ever chocolatey breakfast they have in store for us tomorrow morning."

"He's doing much better! He's doing much better!" Bess's shriek reached Nancy through a fog of sleep. The next thing Nancy knew, someone was bouncing at the foot of her bed.

"Oof!" Groaning, Nancy sat up and rubbed her eyes. "Bess, what's going on?" she mumbled groggily. "Did you just win a million dollars or something?"

"No, but listen to this! I woke up early and couldn't get back to sleep. So after I took a shower, I decided to call the hospital and see how Brock's doing. He's off the critical list! He can even have visitors today! So what are we waiting for?"

George came stumbling into the room in her red T-shirt. "Only one thing could make you so happy, Bess," she said, yawning and ruffling a hand through her short brown curls. "Jake's asked you to marry him."

"Jake? Who cares about Jake?" said Bess, waving away the notion. "I'm talking about *Brock,* George! He's well enough to have visitors! Nancy was just saying we should get over there right away," she added. "I even got Brock's room number. Four twenty-four."

With a resigned sigh, Nancy threw off the covers and got out of bed. "Actually, I never said that, but I do think we should head over there," said Nancy. *"After* breakfast."

Oakwood Hospital turned out to be tiny—so tiny that when Nancy mentioned the purpose of their visit at the reception desk, the receptionist asked, "Are you Nancy Drew?"

"Uh, yes, I am," she answered, a bit taken aback. "How did you know?"

"One of the police officers who was here earlier —Ullman, I think his name was—said it would be okay for you to visit Brock even though you're not a member of the family." The young woman glanced sternly at Bess and George. "He didn't say anything about your friends, though."

"Oh, but we've got to see him!" Bess wailed.

"My associates usually accompany me for every facet of an investigation," Nancy said quickly in her most official-sounding voice.

The receptionist wouldn't bend the rules, though. Taking the pass the young woman gave her, Nancy took the elevator up to the fourth floor.

"Let's see," Nancy murmured aloud, scanning the room numbers as she went down the hall. "Four eighteen—four twenty— There it is."

Brock's room was at the end of the hall. To Nancy's surprise, there was no police officer standing guard outside. Someone was fumbling with the door handle, though—a heavyset man in a lab coat. He half turned at Nancy's approach.

Nancy gasped. It was Dan Avery!

I've got to stop him! an inner voice screeched. He's sneaking in to finish Brock off!

Chapter

Ten

M R. AVERY! What are you doing here?"
Nancy demanded.

Horror filled Dan Avery's face as he turned
and recognized her, but he didn't stop to answer.
Whirling around, he fled rapidly down the corridor.

Nancy dashed after him. Farther down the hall
she glimpsed a burly police officer ambling toward Brock's room with a cup of steaming coffee
in his hand.

"Stop that man!" Nancy shouted, pointing at
Dan Avery. "He was breaking into Brock Sawyer's room!"

Startled, the officer halted in his tracks—and
in that split-second of indecision, Dan Avery
scrambled left down a staircase and disappeared.

Biting off a cry of frustration, Nancy raced

down the hall herself. At the top of the stairs she slid on a slippery patch of floor, nearly colliding with the police officer.

"Hey!" he yelped in pain as scalding coffee spilled onto his hand.

Nancy didn't stop—she continued her race down the steps after Avery. Over the thudding of her heart, she could hear his footsteps pounding down the staircase below her.

Then she heard a woman's voice shouting, "No! That's an emergency exit!"

Too late. Avery had already crashed the emergency door open and gotten away. The shrill beeping of the security system was activated instantly. A moment later Nancy could hear the door slamming shut. When she reached the bottom of the stairs, Avery was gone.

"Oh, no!" Nancy groaned aloud. "I can't believe it!"

"I saw him, miss! I got a good look at him!" A middle-aged woman wearing a pale blue uniform and carrying a can of disinfectant came rushing up to stand at the second-floor landing. "He was a heavyset man, kind of balding," she called to Nancy. "He seemed to be in an awful hurry."

Just then the police officer came skidding into view, panting from exertion. "Just what do you think you're up to, young lady?" he gasped. Then he yelled over his shoulder, "Can't someone please switch off this ridiculous noise?"

A couple of seconds later the security system fell silent.

"Now," the officer began again, glaring at Nancy. "Tell me what's going on."

"I caught that man trying to break into Brock Sawyer's room," she explained. "I think he may be the person who poisoned him."

The police officer—his name tag read Officer Webley, Nancy noticed—gave her a long, dubious look. "And what's *your* connection with Mr. Sawyer?" he asked skeptically. "Fan of his, are you?"

"I'm a private detective." Nancy quickly filled the officer in on her involvement with the case so far. "I haven't seen Dan Avery in the inn since yesterday," she finished. "Whatever he's up to now, it couldn't possibly be good for Brock."

"Well, let's not jump to conclusions," said Officer Webley in a patronizing voice. "Maybe you got mixed up. Whoever you saw going into Mr. Sawyer's room probably works here at the hospital."

"A hospital employee wouldn't run away," Nancy pointed out, trying not to lose her patience. "Anyway, why wasn't there a guard stationed at Brock Sawyer's door? That's pretty loose security for a celebrity like him, isn't it?"

Officer Webley was suddenly uncomfortable. "Uh, I'm supposed to be the guard at the door," he admitted. "I just stepped away for a second to get a cup of coffee. I—uh—I'll check into your story, miss, okay?"

"Okay. But I need to speak to Brock Sawyer, before any more time goes by," she said, showing him her pass.

"Well, I guess a short visit couldn't hurt," the officer said reluctantly after examining the slip of paper.

"Great," said Nancy. "Thank you very much. Oh, and my two associates will be joining me," she added.

"Your associates? Where are they?" Officer Webley looked around as though he expected to see them in the stairwell.

"Down in the lobby waiting for me," Nancy replied. "Why don't you come with me, so you can clear our visit with the receptionist there?"

They found Bess and George looking immensely bored as they scrutinized the gift-shop window in the reception area.

"Is Brock really going to see us?" Bess asked a few minutes later. Officer Webley had spoken with the young woman at reception, and the four of them were riding the elevator back up to the fourth floor. "This is so cool!"

Behind Officer Webley's back, Nancy gave Bess's arm a warning squeeze. "I'm sure he'll be glad to help us with our *investigation*," she said meaningfully. "And I've promised the officer that we won't stay long."

Nancy was relieved that Officer Webley decided to station himself outside the door rather than join them in the room. Otherwise he might have started wondering exactly what kind of a detective Bess was.

"Oh, you poor thing!" Bess cooed, practically flying over to Brock's bedside. "Do you still hurt anywhere? Gosh, it's great to see you again!"

Brock was a little pale, but other than that he seemed to be back to normal. He grinned at Bess from his pile of pillows. Then he waved at Nancy and George, who were pulling over some chairs. "With such a charming cheering squad, it's impossible not to feel better. How are you all doing? And how's Samantha?"

Bess's smile flickered a little. "She's fine. Worried about you—but of course she's got a lot on her mind." Bess's tone somehow managed to convey the suggestion that Samantha was too busy to be thinking much about Brock. "What with this fire and all, she's really—"

"What fire?" Brock cut in. He propped himself up on his elbows, concern making his features look even more rugged than usual.

Nancy filled him in. "Samantha has asked me to investigate the case," she finished. "That's why I wanted to talk to you as soon as I could. We've got to figure out who might want to kill you, Brock."

He leaned back dejectedly against the pillows again. "It sounds so weird to hear you say that," he said. "Until a couple of days ago I didn't know I had any enemies, let alone one who wants me dead! I mean, what could I have done to make anyone so angry?"

"Well, there's something your father did that might have made Mrs. Tagley very angry," Nancy said hesitantly. "Do you know about that?"

"I do, and believe me, I'll never forgive my father for treating another human being that way," he said sincerely.

"But I've already talked about my father with Mrs. Tagley," Brock went on. "About two years ago—at the end of the summer I was dating Samantha—Sam's mother and I hashed the whole thing out."

"You did?" Nancy asked, arching a brow. "She didn't mention that to me."

Brock shrugged. "Maybe that's because she and I agreed to put the whole business out of our minds. It was a terrible thing, but it's over now. I may not be Mrs. Tagley's favorite person, but I'm sure she doesn't hate me enough to poison me."

Nancy mentally flipped through her list of suspects. "What about Tim?" she asked.

A dark look came into Brock's blue eyes. "If I had to put money on anyone, I'd pick Tim as the culprit," he said slowly. "You saw that fight we had, but you haven't seen all the little ways he's tried to provoke me. Making fun of me under his breath, intercepting my phone messages, sending room service to my bedroom at four in the morning. Nothing you can really get mad about, but it's been a real drag. I don't want to sound paranoid, Nancy, but Tim's been against me all along."

"And Jake?" asked Nancy. "There's some evidence that points to him."

Brock was startled. "I thought he was on my side. He's been really nice and polite."

"What about Dan Avery?" asked George.

"Who?" asked Brock blankly.

"A guest named Dan Avery," Nancy explained. "I caught him trying to break into this room half an hour ago. You must have seen him around the inn."

"He's hard to miss," Bess added. "Stumpy-looking, with greasy hair and beady little eyes. Sort of like a sleazy woodchuck."

"Sounds charming," said Brock, chuckling. "I can't wait to meet him. But I don't think I *have* met him yet. Never even heard of him. And I certainly have no idea why he'd want to kill me."

"Well, thanks for your help. We're glad you're better, at least," said Nancy, straightening up. She'd been hoping to come up with more leads, but Brock hadn't added much to what they already knew. "Did you eat or drink anything unusual the night you were poisoned? The chocolates came up clean, you know, so you must have taken the poison in some other food."

"I can't really think of anything," Brock said, shaking his head. "I had exactly what Sam had. In fact, she brought me my plate of food from the buffet line. I was afraid that I'd pig out if I went up there myself."

Nancy, Bess, and George exchanged a quick glance. What Brock had just told them was more important than he realized. If Samantha was the last person to handle Brock's food before he ate it, the finger of suspicion pointed very strongly in her direction now.

But Nancy didn't think she should mention this detail aloud—not until she had more to go on, at least. There was no point in upsetting Brock unnecessarily. "Thanks again for your help" was all she said.

"And we'll come to see you again very soon," Bess added eagerly.

"This case is turning out to be tricky," said Nancy as she and her friends walked out to the parking lot. "I haven't been able to narrow down our list of suspects at all."

"You've never blown a case yet, Nancy," George reminded her. "I'm sure you'll turn up something. You always do."

"Well, I wish I knew where to turn next," Nancy said, half to herself. The three girls had almost reached the row where Nancy's Mustang was parked. "It all seems so—"

Nancy stopped in her tracks. "Look!" she gasped, pointing across the parking lot. "There's Dan Avery!"

He was just unlocking a car door.

"We've got to catch him!" Nancy cried. She and George took off across the lot at the same time.

"This time, he's not going to get away!"

Chapter

Eleven

AT THE SOUND of Nancy's voice, Dan Avery dropped his keys and bolted. This time, though, Nancy had started running before he had—and it was two against one. While Nancy was making a beeline for Avery, George dashed around the other side of the parking lot to head him off. It took only a couple of minutes before they had him trapped.

For a minute it looked as if Avery was going to fight. But while aiming a totally ineffectual punch at Nancy, he slipped and fell flat on his back, and lay there panting from the exertion.

"Help me hold him, George," Nancy gasped, struggling to pin Avery's feet down.

Bess had just caught up to them. "I'll get his arm," she called, panting.

In a few seconds the three girls had Avery totally immobilized.

"And now," Nancy said, *"now* you're going to tell us what's going on."

"No way," said Dan Avery sullenly. "I'm not wasting my time explaining myself to a bunch of hysterical teenage girls. Let me up or I'll report you to the police."

"The police know about you already," said Nancy grimly. "The officer guarding Brock is on the lookout for you right now." It wasn't exactly true, but Avery wasn't in much of a position to question her. "So you might as well talk to us."

Glaring at her, Avery said defiantly, "There's nothing to talk about. I'm just doing my job. And you'll be sorry if you get in the way."

"What are you talking about?" asked Bess incredulously. "Murdering people is your *job?*"

"Murdering people?" Dan Avery stared back at the girls just as incredulously. "What are *you* talking about?"

"Your attempted murder of Brock Sawyer," Nancy answered flatly. "And of me."

Suddenly all the color drained from Dan Avery's face. "Attempted—you suspect *me?*" he sputtered. "You think I . . ." His voice trailed off, and he shook his head wordlessly.

"I'm a reporter," he said at last. "I'm just trying to get a story. I-I'm not a murderer!"

He sounded sincere, but Nancy wasn't convinced. "Maybe you'd better tell us about it, Mr. Avery.

"Sure, sure." Now Dan Avery seemed pathetically eager to comply. "But could you let me up? It's hard to talk when the three of you are pressing me into the asphalt."

Nancy, Bess, and George cautiously took their hands off him and stood up, brushing the dust from their clothes. Rubbing a shaky hand over his sweaty face, their captive got slowly to his feet.

"I'm a reporter with the *Midnight Examiner,*" Avery began. "Well, the *Examiner* is probably the only newspaper in the country that wasn't invited to the Chocolate Festival."

"Wait a minute," said Nancy. "Didn't Brock say something about the *Examiner*—about the stories you've been running on him?"

The stocky reporter nodded. "That's right. We've been giving him a hard time, I guess—but, hey, he's famous. It's the price you pay when you become a star. Anyway, everyone knows the *Examiner*'s not some big, serious paper like the Chicago *Tribune*. It's just a fun read!"

"I guess Brock didn't feel that way about it, though," said George dryly.

"Uh-huh. That's why he warned us to stay away. But my editor thought it would be a great scoop if we could sneak in anyway. A great *scoop.*" His mouth widened into a big smile. "Get it? Like a scoop of chocolate ice cream? It was going to be the headline." He looked from face to face, but none of the three girls was smiling. "Uh, anyway, I knew I'd never get a legit invitation, so I—well, I kind of got one from someone who owed me a favor."

"What do you mean?" Nancy asked warily.

Avery scratched his balding head before answering. "I sort of—persuaded another reporter to give me his invitation. He works for another paper, see, and one time I slipped him a couple of celebrity photos from the *Examiner*'s files when he was in a tight spot. So he owed me.

"So anyway, I sneaked in, using this other guy's invitation. And I've been waiting for a big—er—scoop ever since. His getting dipped in the chocolate was good," he recalled, "but what I was really looking for was a big juicy story about Brock being poisoned. Boy, would our readers go for that!"

Nancy was completely disgusted. It sounded as if he actually enjoyed ruining people's reputations. "So what are you doing here at the hospital?" Nancy asked icily. "Wasn't the story back at the inn juicy enough?"

"Yeah, but I didn't have any pictures. I wasn't there when Brock got zapped—took the poison, I mean. I was—well, to tell you the truth, I was feeling sick to my stomach. Too much chocolate, I guess," said Avery sheepishly. "Since I didn't have any photos from the actual poisoning, I decided that a few shots of Brock in his hospital bed would be the next best thing.

"I've been camping out here for the past day," Avery went on, "waiting for a chance to sneak in. That's what you caught me trying to do a little while ago."

He gave a little shrug. "So there we are. A man's got to earn a living, you know."

"One more question," Nancy told him. "Did you touch any of Brock's food before he got sick? Or his utensils?"

"Uh, actually I did more than touch the guy's food. I helped myself to a little of it. Not really his food," the reporter added hastily. "Just some of that weird artificial sweetener he took around with him. I put some into my coffee at lunchtime when he was busy signing an autograph. I know it sounds dumb, but I wanted to cut a few calories.

"Well, if that's it I guess I'll be going." Dan Avery started off in the direction of his car, but Nancy grabbed his arm.

"Wait a minute," she said suddenly. "You say you took the sweetener at lunchtime, Mr. Avery?"

He nodded.

"And you were feeling sick at dinnertime?"

"More than sick!" Avery said emphatically. "I mean, I was—ah—really indisposed all afternoon."

"Then it might be the sweetener!" said Nancy excitedly. "If it made you sick, it could have poisoned Brock. This could be the break I've been looking for!"

George was looking at her curiously. "So someone put the poison in the sweetener?"

"That's got to be it!" Nancy exclaimed. "Let's get going, guys. Bess and George, could you head back to the inn and see if you can track down that jar of sweetener? Maybe Mr. Avery could give you a ride back—"

"Be delighted to," said the reporter with a big grin. "It's the least I can do."

Behind him Bess was giving Nancy a disgusted look that said "thanks for nothing."

"Where are *you* going, Nan?" George asked.

"To the police lab," she replied. "The lab technicians and I are going to have a little chat. About poison."

"I think I can get you in to see Dr. Demado," said a young man at the reception desk. He led Nancy down the hall to an office.

Dr. Demado turned out to be a calm, gray-haired woman in a business suit. "Of course I've heard of the Oakwood case," she said when Nancy explained why she'd come. "Calomel poisoning, right? As far as I know, we haven't traced the source yet."

"But I've just found something out." Nancy went on to tell Dr. Demado what she'd learned from Dan Avery.

The chemist whistled. "No wonder he felt so sick! A dose of calomel could really lay a person flat."

"But how could one poison have caused two such different reactions?" Nancy inquired.

"Calomel definitely could," Dr. Demado said with a firm nod. "Do you remember what Brock was using the sweetener for?"

"Iced tea," Nancy told her. "Iced tea with lemon. And coffee. I saw him use the sweetener in that, too."

"Calomel breaks down into a poison when it

comes into contact with acid," Dr. Demado explained. "Acid like the lemon in Brock Sawyer's tea."

"*And* in the chocolates he tasted," Nancy suddenly remembered, growing more excited. "They were lemon truffles. And he ate two of them before he collapsed."

"So he got a double dose of acid," Dr. Demado mused, shaking her head.

"Wait a minute," said Nancy. "Let me catch up to you." Rapidly she summarized what she'd heard so far.

"Someone dumped calomel into Brock's artificial sweetener. Brock and Mr. Avery both used the sweetener, but neither of them noticed that it had been poisoned because calomel is tasteless. It made Mr. Avery fall sick because that's what calomel does. But it poisoned Brock because he took it with the acid in his tea and in those lemon truffles. Is that right?"

"Right."

There was still one piece missing from the puzzle, Nancy realized. "But where would someone get calomel?" she asked.

"Now, that's something I can't answer," said the chemist. "It was taken off the market as an internal medicine years ago—precisely because it was so unstable. Possibly your poisoner found it in an old medicine cabinet somewhere?"

Nancy nodded, remembering the walk she, Bess, and George had taken through the inn's east wing. Some of the rooms there had looked as if they'd been left untouched for years—

including a couple of bathrooms. It wasn't uncommon for people to hold on to old medicines they should have thrown out. So the poisoner might have been able to dig up calomel pretty easily—

Abruptly Nancy thought of something else. "Wait," she said aloud. "Would the poisoner have known Brock was going to be eating something with acid in it? Those truffles were kept secret until Samantha unveiled them. Besides, is there anyone at the inn who knows that calomel turns into a poison when it reacts with acid? That seems a little hard to believe. . . ."

Nancy slumped down in her chair as her excitement drained away. "Whoever put calomel into Brock's sweetener may not have meant to kill him at all," she said in despair.

Dr. Demado eyed her curiously. "Why is that bad?" she asked.

"Oh, in terms of the poisoner's guilt, it's not bad at all," Nancy said quickly. "But if it's true, it means I've got to start looking for a different motive.

"I've been on the wrong track all along!"

Chapter

Twelve

As NANCY DROVE BACK to the inn, she hardly noticed the scenery. Her mind was circling around the newest development in the case.

From the poisoner's point of view, putting calomel in Brock's artificial sweetener made a lot of sense. No one else would take it. He or she could be guaranteed that at some point Brock would use it.

But Nancy was sure that even the poisoner didn't know that calomel would turn into a poison when it reacted with the lemon juice in the tea and the truffles. After all, Nancy knew a fair amount about poisons—more than the average person, at least. And she had never even heard of calomel, much less that it could turn poisonous in the presence of acid!

No, whoever had used the calomel had probably intended to make Brock feel sick—*and* to ruin the truffle-tasting event. If that was true, that person's goal *might* be to sabotage the festival—not to kill Brock.

So I'm back to square one, Nancy thought, banging the steering wheel in frustration. She had to figure out who would want the Chocolate Festival to fail. Quickly she ran down her list of suspects again.

Perhaps Samantha had found the stress of running the festival to be too much. She might have decided to end it any way she could.

Mrs. Tagley had a motive for wanting the festival to end, too. She seemed to feel that she and Samantha were in direct competition for control of her inn. Ruining the festival would be a good way to make Samantha look as if she couldn't handle things without her mother.

Then there was Tim. He had every reason to resent the demands the festival was making on Samantha's time.

"On top of that," Nancy said aloud, "there may be suspects I haven't started suspecting yet—a whole inn full of them."

"No sign of Brock's sweetener," George announced when Nancy let herself into the girls' suite a short while later. She had spread her lean frame out on the couch and had a book propped up on her stomach. "We hunted through the kitchen until the chef was ready to wring our necks. But it's gone."

"Jake even pitched in and helped for a while," Bess called from her room, where she was lying on her bed with a magazine. "You know, he's really a sweet guy. I wonder if I'm making a mistake concentrating on Brock so much."

"It probably doesn't make much difference, considering that your relationship with Brock is completely in your head," said George.

"We've got to find that jar of sweetener," said Nancy. "It could be the key to everything." She recounted what Dr. Demado had told her.

"So we're not dealing with poison, we're dealing with sabotage," said George, her brown eyes wide.

"That's right," answered Nancy. "We've got to determine who hates the Chocolate Festival enough to ruin it." She let out a sigh. "We don't know whether the culprit used the calomel because it was the first thing he or she came across, or whether he or she chose it on purpose.

"We don't even know for sure that the calomel was *in* the sweetener," she added. "That's why we've got to find that jar."

Nancy started pacing around the little room. "While everyone's busy with the festival, I'm going to check all the Tagleys' rooms for it."

"What if someone walks in on you? What are you going to say?" Bess asked nervously, getting off her bed and joining Nancy and George in the living room.

"That's not going to happen," Nancy told her with a grin. "Because you and George are going

111

to be my lookouts. I know you'll be great at fending people off while I'm poking around under the Tagleys' beds."

"We'd better come up with some kind of excuse, don't you think?" Bess whispered a few minutes later as the three girls headed toward the stairs that led up a flight to the Tagleys' suite of rooms. The fourth-floor hall was hushed and shadowy. Nancy felt as if they were in the middle of a ghost story.

"Maybe I can say I dropped an earring—" Bess suggested.

"And it just rolled up four flights into the Tagleys' wing?" George finished for her. "I doubt they'll go for that. If anyone comes up here, let's just try to distract them."

Nancy held her breath as she twisted the knob of the first door they came to. It swung open easily.

"Thank heaven for friendly family inns like this one," said George with a chuckle.

"What a pretty bedroom!" Bess commented.

It was furnished entirely in antique cherry furniture, and on the floor was a faded but still handsome Oriental rug. From the framed pictures of Samantha and Jake that lined the walls, Nancy guessed this was Mr. and Mrs. Tagley's room.

"Look, this must have been taken when Jake was about four years old," said Bess, pointing to a picture of a sunny-faced little boy in a cowboy suit. "What a cutie!"

"Hey, get outside," scolded Nancy with a

laugh. "You guys are supposed to be standing guard, remember?"

"Oops, sorry!" Bess scooted out of the room to stand with George.

Nancy quickly searched the room. No sweetener in the closet or any of the bureau drawers. None under the bed or any of the furniture, nor in the medicine cabinet of the bathroom adjoining the bedroom. After a few minutes she decided she was wasting her time.

"No luck," she said, closing the door carefully behind her. "Let's try another room."

To her relief, the next door they tried was also unlocked. This room was obviously Jake's.

"What a mess!" George marveled, staring at the piles of books and magazines on the floor. The desk was cluttered with papers, and the unmade bed was piled high with laundry. "Anyone who wanted to break in here would give up and leave, thinking someone had already beat him to it."

Nancy gave George a friendly jab on the shoulder.

Nancy sifted through piles of wadded-up shirts, peered cautiously around precariously balanced stacks of books, and dug mountains of debris out from under the bed before shoving them back again. The whole search would have been a lot easier if she had dared to clean up the room, but, of course, that was impossible.

She had just decided to give up when Bess leaned into the room. "Nancy, hurry!" she begged. "You've been in there for ten minutes!"

"Okay. I'm done—at least, I think I am. There may still be a pile of laundry I didn't paw through, but I don't think so."

"Couldn't you just skip Samantha's room?" urged Bess. "I'm sure she didn't take the jar. I just know someone's going to discover us any minute. And besides, it's lunchtime!"

"I can't quit now." Leading the way, Nancy rounded a corner onto a sunny corridor lined with windows. Seeing another door there, Nancy tried it.

Unlike Jake's, Samantha's room was in pristine order, with a dainty canopy bed and white-painted furniture.

"This won't take long, anyway," Nancy muttered to herself as she began pulling out bureau drawers.

"Come *on*, Nancy!" Bess urged. She was dancing up and down with impatience. "You're taking forever!"

"It's only been about three minutes," Nancy protested as she pulled open the closet door. "Just give me a chance to—"

Nancy froze.

"Oh, no," she whispered.

Tucked into the back of the closet, behind a pair of leather tennis shoes, was the jar of sweetener.

Chapter

Thirteen

Nᴀɴᴄʏ ᴘɪᴄᴋᴇᴅ ᴜᴘ the small jar and hurried back into the hall. "Guys, I hit the jackpot!"

Bess's mouth fell open. "In Samantha's room? I don't believe it." In her surprise she seemed to forget they could be found out any minute. But George grabbed her arm and dragged her down the hall.

A minute later they were back in their suite with the door safely shut. Bess plopped down on the couch. "I just don't believe she put that jar there, Nan," she said again. "Someone's framing her. Why would she hold on to something so incriminating? Besides, Samantha wouldn't poison a guy she used to be in love with."

Nancy went to get her purse from her room and tucked the jar of sweetener safely inside. "I hope you're right, Bess."

"I hope so, too," said George. "But how are you going to prove it, Nan?"

"I'm not sure. Right after lunch I'll take the jar to the police lab. I want them to tell me whether it's actually got calomel in it before I start talking to Samantha." She checked her watch. "We're already late. We'd better get down to the dining room."

"You were right, Nancy," said Officer Sherbinski, coming into the waiting area of the police lab. She held up the jar of sweetener Nancy had given her. "This sweetener *has* been laced with calomel. I'm afraid this may implicate Samantha."

Nancy nodded. She'd been waiting for the better part of the afternoon, but it had been worth it.

"By the way, Tim Krueger has been released," the technician added.

"Why? Lack of evidence?" Nancy asked.

The officer nodded. "This jar of poisoned sweetener is our best evidence."

"It's not enough to arrest Samantha, though," Nancy put in quickly.

"No. But it gives us a very good reason to question her further."

After thanking Officer Sherbinski, Nancy went back outside.

If I could only find the jar of calomel itself! she

thought as she climbed into her car and switched on the ignition. But whoever had found the calomel originally had surely gotten rid of it by now. But then Nancy would have thought the poisoner would have thrown the sweetener away, too.

It was almost six-thirty by the time Nancy reached the inn again. When she opened the door to her suite, Bess and George weren't there, but something else was. Nancy saw that a note with her name on it had been slipped under the door. It was printed on cheap stationery that had been folded in half. Nancy unfolded it and read the message inside.

If you want to know more about the poison, meet me in the east wing at 7:00 P.M. tonight.

It was signed "A Friend."

The handwriting was utterly without character. Nancy couldn't begin to guess whether it had been written by a man or a woman.

Note in hand, Nancy walked toward her bedroom. What the—

She hurried over to her bed and snatched up a second piece of paper. This note was from Bess and George.

Nan,
We're down in the dining room. Don't skip dinner just for a case! Meet us there!

B & G

Nancy grinned to herself. She *was* going to skip dinner. But she'd slip down to the dining room first to ask them to cover for her.

But Nancy didn't get to leave the dining room as fast as she'd planned.

"Tim!" Nancy exclaimed. He was walking toward the Tagleys' table arm in arm with Samantha.

"It's great to be back," Tim said warmly. "I never would have thought I'd miss the Chocolate Festival. But it only takes a second or two of being in police custody to make you appreciate what you've got."

"When did they release you?" Nancy asked.

It was Samantha who answered. "Last night," she said happily, giving his arm a squeeze. "He's had a twenty-four-hour vacation from the festival, so now he's extra-ready to help me out again." She leaned teasingly against her boyfriend and ruffled his dark hair. "Aren't you? Now can we please eat? I'm starving."

They continued on to the table, but Nancy stayed rooted where she was. A horrible thought had just struck her.

"Nancy! The appetizers are on their way!"

Bess's voice shook her back to reality—sort of. She started toward her friends, who were sitting at a table by themselves.

"And they'll be a lot more appetizing if they're *not* made of chocolate," said George as Nancy reached the table and pulled out a chair. "I'm getting a little sick of eating dessert before my main course—"

Suddenly she stopped speaking and peered more closely at Nancy. "What's the matter, Nan?"

"I just talked to Tim," Nancy said.

"But—but it's great that he's not being held anymore, isn't it?" Bess asked.

"Yes," Nancy said slowly, "but he was released last night—not today."

"So?" Bess bit into a chocolate-iced roll.

"So he could have been the one who poured that flour all over me. He had plenty of time."

"Oh, no," said George. "I was really hoping Tim wasn't a suspect."

"Me, too," Nancy agreed. "But I guess we can't rule him out yet." She sighed. "This is terrible. I have too many suspects!"

"Maybe eating something will make you feel better," suggested Bess.

Nancy shook her head. "No, thanks. I'm not eating. I've got a rendezvous instead."

"A rendezvous?" echoed George.

In a low voice Nancy explained.

"Nan, you can't meet a total stranger," Bess protested in a worried voice. "It could be the murderer!"

"What murderer?" asked Nancy. "No one's dead that I know of. It's probably just someone who wants to tell me something about the case in a place where we're not likely to be overheard. Now, come on. Can you guys really see me *not* meeting this person, whoever it is?"

Both of her friends shook their heads.

"Would you guys cover for me again?" Nancy

asked. "If anyone asks for me, don't tell them what I'm doing, okay?"

"No problem," George assured her. "Want us to save you something to eat?"

"No, thanks. I can call room service later." Nancy chuckled. "Maybe Mrs. Reames will have some more gossip for me."

If the Tagleys' living quarters had been a little creepy, the east wing at night was positively frightening. The moonlight streaming through the windows gave the only light. It shone down onto the huge, empty rooms filled with signs of construction—ladders, scaffolding, cans of joint compound and paint, and ghostly white tarpaulins draped here and there.

Nancy shuddered. Don't get nervous, she reminded herself. You're here for a reason. But she still didn't know exactly where in the east wing she was to meet her invisible "friend."

Nancy squared her shoulders resolutely as she walked from one dark, deserted room to another. She was so determined to stay calm that when the noise first sounded, she told herself she hadn't heard a thing.

But then it happened again. And this time Nancy knew she wasn't imagining things.

It was a soft, gentle tapping. In broad daylight it would have sounded like nothing more than a child knocking on a door. In the darkness it sounded like a ghostly summons beckoning Nancy forward.

"Stop it," Nancy scolded herself aloud. "It's just the floors settling or something."

Tap tap . . . tap tap . . . tap tap . . .

No, that was too regular to be the floors. Someone was making that sound. Could it possibly be a signal luring her to the meeting?

Nancy tiptoed toward the doorway of the vast, empty room she was standing in and poked her head out into the corridor. There was no doubt about it—the sound was coming from down the hall.

Moving as silently as she could, Nancy slipped down the hall. Always the tapping seemed just a few feet ahead of her, but she couldn't seem to reach it. She followed the sound down the hall, around the corner, and into yet another shadowy room. Then, abruptly, there was silence.

Nancy took a tentative step forward—and froze in fear.

Just in front of her the room's floor had been ripped out. The space was like a bottomless black pit. A few more steps, and she would have plunged into it!

Nancy's heart was pounding. I've been led into a trap! Someone lured me here to—

Just then there was a scrabbling sound behind her. Nancy whirled around—and screamed.

From out of the darkness a razor-sharp wood chisel was hurtling straight at her!

Chapter

Fourteen

No!" NANCY SCREAMED. She jumped out of the chisel's deadly path and felt as if someone had pulled the floor out from under her. She was plummeting through the gaping hole!

It all happened in a flash. Almost before she realized she was falling, Nancy's flailing arms had grabbed a beam and she jerked still. Gasping for breath, she clung to the beam. She didn't dare look down. Below her, she knew, yawned the cavernous space of the subbasement. The only thing that would keep her from smashing to the stone floor below was her own strength —and already her muscles were shrieking with agony.

As the panic subsided, she realized something was stabbing into her hand—probably a nail sticking out from the beam. Carefully Nancy moved her hand a fraction to the right. Better. Then, warily, she raised her eyes.

She couldn't hear her assailant anywhere. Was he—or she—lurking above her, waiting for her to drop? Waiting to kick her hands off the beam if she made a move?

Nancy suddenly remembered something else. The chisel! She desperately searched her memory to see whether she had heard it drop through the floor, but she couldn't remember. Had her attacker found it? Was the chisel poised to strike again?

She listened again—and heard no sign of anyone else nearby.

I can't hang here forever, Nancy told herself. Even if someone *was* up there, the risks of climbing back up were a lot better than what would happen if she dropped into the subbasement.

But getting up on the beam was easier said than done. It took three agonizing tries before Nancy was able to hoist herself onto it. Precariously balanced, and feeling as if she might fall with every movement, she began to creep to safety.

The hand that had been pierced by the nail was throbbing now, and her muscles ached. Nancy felt sick with pain and fear. But inch by dreadful inch she moved along until at last she had reached the edge of the hole.

Trembling with relief, she crawled onto solid ground and collapsed onto the floor. For a minute all she could do was lie sprawled against the floor, breathing deeply. Then she pulled herself together and sat up.

She peered down the shadowy hallway. There was neither sight nor sound of her attacker. Whoever had set this trap was gone.

That had been a close call. But if her assailant thought she'd back off now, he—or she—had another think coming!

Trying to kill her that way had been a desperate move. And now that the culprit was desperate, it was time for Nancy to make her own move—one that would send the criminal over the edge.

"Nancy, you missed the best mocha sorbet—" Bess's smile turned to a look of shock. "What happened to you?"

Nancy had come directly to the dining room from the east wing. Luckily the dining room was nearly empty now. But a few late diners were staring at Nancy's dusty clothes and bloody hands. At least the Tagleys, Samantha, and Tim were gone, Nancy noted with relief.

"You look as though you've been crawling through construction or something," George added.

"That's pretty much what I *have* been doing," said Nancy wearily as she dropped into a chair. "I'll fill you in in a second. Just let me catch my breath."

"Did you meet whoever sent you that note?" asked George.

"Well, yes and no. I think that now it's time to get tough."

"How?" Bess asked.

Just then a waiter walked up to the table. "Can I get you anything?" he asked Nancy politely.

"Just some information. Were you working here when Brock Sawyer was poisoned?"

"No, but another waiter on duty tonight was. Do you want me to get him?"

"That would be great."

A young waiter with dark, spiky hair appeared shortly. "Do you have time to talk to me for a second?" Nancy asked him.

"I guess so," he answered with a quick glance around the dining room. "Things seem to be winding down here."

"Thanks a lot. This won't take long," Nancy assured him. "I understand you were on duty when Brock Sawyer was poisoned?"

"I was. What a horrible thing!"

"It looks now as though an artificial sweetener that Brock used in his tea and coffee was what poisoned him," Nancy went on.

The waiter's eyes grew wide. "You mean that powdery stuff? Boy, I'm glad I didn't try any! I never trust health food."

Nancy couldn't help laughing a little. "Actually, someone *added* the poison to the sweetener," she explained. "That's what I'm trying to find out. You didn't notice anyone besides Brock handling the jar of sweetener, did you?"

The waiter thought for a moment. "Besides Mr. Tagley, you mean?"

"Mr. Tagley?" Nancy asked incredulously.

"Jake, that is. He likes the staff to call him Mr. Tagley."

"I didn't realize that," Nancy said, half to herself.

"Well, anyway, Mr. Tagley took it out to the kitchen. Day before yesterday, I'm pretty sure. He said it needed a refill."

Nancy shot her friends a meaningful glance. That was the day Brock was poisoned.

"Do they keep refills of Brock's sweetener in the kitchen?" asked George in surprise.

"I've never seen any," the waiter said, shrugging, "but Jake must know the kitchen a lot better than I do. He came back with the refill right away." The waiter glanced at the clock on the opposite wall. "I should really get back," he said. With a quick smile, he walked away.

"Let's go upstairs," Nancy said to Bess and George as soon as the waiter was out of earshot. "We'll be able to talk a lot more easily without people leaning over our shoulders."

"So Jake refilled the sweetener," Nancy mused thoughtfully when the girls were in the elevator heading upstairs. "I wonder if—"

"You're not accusing him of being the poisoner, are you?" Bess cut in. "Because I just know he's not."

Nancy smiled slightly. "If it were up to you, Bess, no one would be the culprit." The elevator door slid open, and the girls started down the third-floor hallway. As soon as they reached their suite, Nancy began peeling off her grimy clothes.

"Anyway, I'm not accusing Jake of anything,"

Nancy continued. "It does seem significant that he handled the sweetener just before Brock was poisoned. But I've got to take a shower and put some disinfectant on my hand before I even *think* about this case."

Fifteen minutes later—showered, dressed in clean shorts and a T-shirt, and feeling a hundred percent better—Nancy sat down in the suite's living room with Bess and George and told them what had just happened to her.

Bess's blue eyes were full of tears when Nancy finished. "Nan, you could have been killed!"

George didn't seem to even hear her cousin. Her brow was furrowed as she asked, "Remember the night we saw Jake playing darts?"

Nancy nodded. "So?"

"So someone aimed that chisel pretty well, that's all," George answered.

"You're right!" Nancy exclaimed. "I didn't even think of that, George!"

Bess was angry. "You don't have a shred of proof, either of you!" she stated emphatically.

"That's right, we don't," agreed Nancy. "That's why I came up with a new plan while I was in the shower. It ought to help us even if we *don't* have any proof."

"Well, what *is* this plan?" asked George. "How can we help?"

"First, did you guys notice anyone in the Tagley family leave the dining room during dinner?" said Nancy.

"Let's see," George said thoughtfully. "They were all in and out. Weren't they, Bess?"

"Except Jake," Bess said with a triumphant smile. "He came in a couple of minutes late, then stayed for the whole meal. But both Mr. and Mrs. Tagley left a couple of times, and so did Samantha. Come to think of it, Tim did, too. He was bringing in some kind of speaker system for the dance tonight. I think we should definitely go to that, by the way. It'll probably be fun."

"I doubt we'll have time to get to the dance," Nancy said apologetically. "I have a feeling we're going to be busy this evening.

"But I've got to make one call to set things up for my plan," Nancy went on. She opened the local directory that lay next to the phone on the coffee table and looked up the number of the hospital. Then she picked up the receiver and began to dial.

"Hello, may I please speak to Brock Sawyer?" she said when the hospital switchboard answered. After a short pause the actor's voice came on the line.

"Hello, Brock? This is Nancy Drew. . . . Fine, thank you. And you? . . . Oh, that's good. Listen, Brock. I've come up with a plan to trap the person who poisoned you, but I'm going to need your help. And I think I'm going to need a doctor's permission, too."

A few minutes later Nancy hung up and turned excitedly to her friends. "Now we'll run through my plan—and then we start rehearsing."

The living room clock was just striking nine as Nancy walked gravely into the room and closed the double doors behind her. Waiting for her were Bess, George, and the group of people who had assembled at Nancy's request.

Mrs. Tagley was there, sitting on the faded love seat by the fireplace. Samantha leaned against one wall, worriedly fingering the silk of her blue dress. Tim sat in a chair next to her, his head in his hands. And Jake made a determined effort to flip through a magazine despite the tension in the room.

From far down the hall the lilting strains of ballroom music could be heard.

Samantha checked her watch. "The dance has already started," she said. "I hope you can let me get back soon, Nancy. I don't want to leave my stepfather to run things there too long without me."

"Would you mind telling me what's going on, Nancy?" Mrs. Tagley asked angrily. "I've got a lot of work to do, too, you know!" She began tapping her high heel impatiently on the floor.

"I'm sure Nancy's got a good reason for bringing us all together," said Jake.

"Well, I hope we're not in for some kind of interrogation," Tim muttered. Samantha shot him a warning glance, but he ignored it. "I've answered enough questions in the past couple of days."

"I haven't come to interrogate you. I've come with some news," Nancy told them. "News from the hospital." Her voice was so somber that the group fell still instantly. Every pair of eyes in the room was watching Nancy intently.

Nancy made her voice tremble as she spoke again. "I just talked to Brock's doctor," she said. "He told me that Brock has had a relapse."

Samantha let out a little gasp. "But I—I spoke to him on the phone earlier. He was fine!"

"It happened very quickly." Nancy bit her lip and stared at the floor as though she were fighting to keep from crying. Then she took a deep breath and said the hardest thing of all.

"An hour ago Brock Sawyer died."

Chapter
Fifteen

THERE WAS A GASP of horror from Nancy's listeners.

"Oh, no! Oh, no!" Samantha cried sharply. "It's my fault! If only I hadn't asked Brock to come here!" Burying her head in her hands, she burst into tears.

Tim patted her shoulder awkwardly, but his green eyes showed no emotion. Nancy wondered fleetingly what he was thinking. What would it feel like to console your girlfriend over another guy's death?

Mrs. Tagley was sitting as if paralyzed, her face so pale that Nancy was afraid she was going to faint. And Jake was biting his lip as if he, too, feared that he might cry.

There were tears in Bess's eyes as well. "I—I

131

can't believe it," she said in a trembling voice. "I thought he was doing so much better!"

Great acting, Bess! Nancy cheered silently. In a sober voice she said aloud, "He was. But the doctor says his system was so weak that when he ran a fever, his body couldn't hold out against it."

"Then that makes it murder we're dealing with, doesn't it?" asked George, her brown eyes wide as she looked around the room. "Now that Brock is dead, one of these people is a murderer," she said in a hushed tone.

"That's right," said Nancy. She, too, eyed the roomful of people. "One of you is Brock's killer."

Mrs. Tagley shook her head in disgust. "This is all a little melodramatic, isn't it?" she asked harshly. "Do you suspect one of us in particular, or did you just bring us together for the fun of it?"

"You're all suspects," Nancy replied. "And since you started this conversation, Mrs. Tagley, I'll start with you."

Taking a few steps toward Samantha's mother, Nancy said, "From the very beginning there seemed to be two different ways to read this case. It was possible that someone was out to sabotage the Chocolate Festival. It was also possible that someone was out to get Brock. In your case, Mrs. Tagley, sabotage was unlikely. But there was a good reason you might be out to get Brock."

Nancy met the older woman's glare steadily. "In fact, you probably had the strongest motive of anyone in this room," she said. "Brock's father ruined your first husband's life. You could even say he killed him."

Samantha turned to stare at her mother. "You never told me that!" she breathed.

"It wasn't worth telling," Mrs. Tagley answered in a strained voice. "It was all in the past."

"But was it?" Nancy continued. "Your life was very difficult for a long time after Mr. Patton's death. Any sane person would feel a grudge toward the son of someone who'd inflicted such a terrible wound."

"But he and I talked that whole mess over," Mrs. Tagley burst out, her face red. "Brock wasn't my favorite person, but I would never have poisoned him!"

"That's what you say now," said Nancy. "But I'm not sure I believe you.

"You had a strong motive, too, Tim," she went on, turning to face him. "Jealousy *is* one of the most common motives for murder. You could see that Brock's feelings for Samantha hadn't disappeared—and that her feelings for *him* might be stronger than she thought."

Tim just stared sullenly at the floor, but Samantha cried, "No! I was just being polite!"

Nancy paid no attention. "You also had reasons for wanting to sabotage the Chocolate Festival," she told Tim. "It was eating up a huge amount of Samantha's time. Maybe you were jealous of the festival instead of being jealous of Brock. Maybe you poisoned Brock without actually wanting him to die."

Tim raised his head to glare at her. "You're being ridiculous," he growled. "I thought you were a lot smarter than this, Nancy. Anyone who would come up with such a stupid solution has to be pretty dumb."

"I didn't say it was *the* solution," Nancy reminded him. "I just said it *might* be."

Now Nancy turned to Jake. "Jealousy might be your motive, too. I couldn't help noticing that even though you've been very helpful all week, it's Samantha who gets most of the attention in your family."

Samantha and her mother flinched guiltily at that, Nancy noticed.

"You've had some good ideas over the past few days—ideas everyone has ignored," Nancy continued. "Has it been too hard for you being around a stepsister whose rank at the inn is so much higher than yours? Did you feel left out in the cold?"

Jake was stunned. "I didn't *think* I did," he said at last. "I mean, sure Samantha's done a lot better than I have—but she's already graduated from hotel school. When it's my turn, I'm sure I'll do just as well. And as for Sam getting more of the attention"—he smiled crookedly—"well, that's just the way families are. Dad gets less attention than my stepmother. He and I are just background people, I guess."

Glancing toward the love seat, Nancy thought she saw Mrs. Tagley's stern veneer crack once more. "You're not background people to me," Mrs. Tagley said, dabbing at her eyes.

"And, Samantha—" Nancy wanted to be professional, but she couldn't help speaking more gently to Samantha than she had to the other suspects. "It's hard to believe that you would try to hurt Brock *or* sabotage your own festival. But I've been wondering whether you might have cracked under all the pressure. Was it too much for you? Did you decide you had to put a stop to the whole thing—without losing face?"

Samantha's expression was more hurt than angry. "I—I can see why you'd think that, Nancy," she faltered, staring down at her clasped hands. "What you say—what everyone has been saying—is true. Running the festival *has* been too much for me."

Then, as if she remembered the reason they had all been brought to the library, she stared defiantly up at Nancy. "Still, I'm not guilty of those dumb, vicious pranks, and—and I'm especially not guilty of killing Brock. You'll just have to believe me."

"I wish I *could* believe all of you," Nancy said quietly. "Unfortunately, I can't. One of you is lying.

"Luckily someone has offered to help the liar come forward with the truth," Nancy continued. She turned to the living room doors. "Here he is now."

The handle turned, and the doors pushed slowly open. Brock Sawyer stepped into the room.

"I've come to see justice done," he announced in a solemn voice.

135

Never in her life had Nancy heard a sound like the eerie, shrieking wail that rose from Jake Tagley's lips at that moment.

Jake jumped to his feet, staring wild-eyed at Brock. His cheek was twitching uncontrollably, and sweat was pouring down his face.

"No! No!" he screamed. "Don't come near me! Or I-I'll kill you again!"

Still making that unearthly noise, he stumbled across the library and out the door.

"Well," Brock said. "That has to be the best acting I've ever done."

"You're—you're not dead!" Samantha rushed over to hug Brock, laughing and crying at the same time.

Mrs. Tagley rose shakily to her feet. "Then it was Jake who—who—"

"I'm afraid so," said Nancy urgently. "And now we have to find him because I think he may be dangerous."

Bess, George, and Tim were already on their feet racing out the door.

"There he is!" Bess cried, pointing down the hall. Jake was just disappearing down the stairs to the basement.

Nancy and Tim thundered down the hall after him, shooting past the dining room. The ballroom music that floated out into the hallway sounded horribly out of place.

When they reached the stairs, Nancy took them two at a time.

"He went that way!" Tim shouted, pointing right. "Toward his father's workroom!"

That's strange, Nancy thought. Why run to a place where we can corner him?

But there was no time to think about that. In a flash they had reached the doorway to the store-room.

"Don't come any closer!" Jake screamed.

His four pursuers froze just inside the room.

Jake was just yanking his father's circular saw off its stand, the long electric cord still plugged into the wall outlet. He pressed the On switch and held the saw, whirring ominously, up in the air.

Then—with a taunting smile on his face—he moved it up to a pipe on the wall.

"That looks like a gas pipe!" Tim shouted hoarsely.

"Right you are." Jake gave a mirthless laugh and inched the saw closer to the pipe. "It's the main gas line, and I'm going to saw through it now," he growled.

"But you can't!" George cried. "The sparks will ignite the gas!"

"Right again. The sparks will ignite the gas." The whirring blade was only a fraction of an inch from the pipe now.

"And then," Jake went on, "this whole building will go up in a fireball."

Chapter
Sixteen

I'VE GOT TO stall him! Nancy thought desperately. It's our only hope!

Forcing a light tone into her voice, she said, "I hope you're not planning to kill us before you explain how you pulled this off." She had to talk loudly to be heard over the whirring of the saw. "That would be a little unfair, don't you think?"

Jake gave her an icy stare. "The old stall-the-bad-guy ploy, huh?" he said, to Nancy's dismay. "Well, it won't work. I've seen too many detective movies. Besides," he added bitterly, "I *didn't* pull it off. You tricked me into confessing. Old Jake messed up yet again."

"Oh, stop feeling sorry for yourself," Bess said behind Nancy. "You did a fantastic job. Anyone would have freaked out when Brock walked in like that. I practically had a heart attack myself."

Good, Bess! Nancy thought. Keep it up!

But Jake wasn't going to fall for that trick either.

Scowling, he said, "You're the last person I'd listen to, you traitor. I thought you liked me, not Brock! I should have known I was only your second choice— Well, I'm used to second place now. After all, I'm always second to Samantha."

"I'm surprised to hear you say that," George spoke up. "It seemed to me you were doing as much to keep the inn going as she was. I mean, look at the way you met us at the door when we first got here."

Out of the corner of her eye, Nancy could see Tim edging slowly toward the door.

"Yeah, but did I get any credit for meeting you?" Jake spat out. "No! Samantha acts like she doesn't even want me around!" Nancy could see Jake had gotten even more worked up. "Boy, when I think of the times she's insulted me—and I've just smiled and pretended not to care— Well, I'll pay her back now."

"You certainly will," said Nancy—and she meant it. "I've got to congratulate you, Jake. I thought you *really* didn't care. You always seemed to be so reasonable about everything. You were always calm when everyone else was going crazy."

Tim was standing in the doorway now, poised to slip out into the hall.

"It's not hard to stay calm when you know you're about to get even in a big way," said Jake. "I've been planning this a long time. It doesn't

139

even matter that you caught me, Nancy. I'll die in this fire, but so will everybody else. I think that's a pretty fair trade-off." He lifted the saw toward the pipe again.

"Oh, come on," Bess coaxed. "You've got to tell us how you did all this. I already knew you were smart, but don't you want everyone else to know?"

To Nancy's astonishment, that seemed to do the trick. Jake kept one hand poised on the handle of the saw—but he let go of the On button and lowered the saw to its stand. He didn't seem to notice that Tim was gone.

"Okay, okay," he said. "What do you want to hear before I torch you?"

"Everything," said Nancy promptly. "Start at the beginning. You rigged the scale, didn't you?"

Jake chuckled. "Of course I did. That was hilarious. Seeing Mr. Beautiful chocolate-coated really made my day. Plus I knew my stepmother would give Samantha a lot of grief for it—which is mainly what I wanted. Messing up Brock was secondary to wrecking the festival."

"Well, that was a good start," George said approvingly. "You grossed out a lot of people."

"Yeah, but the ants were even better, don't you think?" said Jake.

Nancy shuddered. "They really were. Where did you ever find so many?"

"I just bought a few ant farms," said Jake offhandedly. "I poured all the ants into a jar—

they came in these little packets—and hid them in the back of the refrigerator. You know that old joke about how no one ever knows what's back there? Well, that's even more true in a big restaurant refrigerator.

"I went out to the kitchen to help bring in some dishes," Jake went on. "When no one was looking, I opened the jar and dumped the ants all over the cake. That wasn't too hard. The cake was already set up on that rolling table, with the cloth over it. So I knew my surprise wouldn't be ruined. Pretty slick, huh?"

Nancy nodded. "Very. But the sweetener was your biggest project of all, of course. You must have found the calomel when you were working in the east wing—is that right?"

"Right," Jake said proudly. "It was in an old medicine cabinet. I read the label and thought, What a weird thing—medicine that's *supposed* to make you sick to your stomach! Then I realized it might be kind of funny to make Brock sick. Especially when he kept blabbing on about that stupid nutritionist with her stupid sweetener. I thought it would really serve him right when his sweetener made him sick!"

"So you didn't mean to poison him?" said Bess. "Oh, I'm so relieved!"

"No, I didn't. When I added the calomel to his sweetener in the kitchen, I had no idea he'd react that way. To tell you the truth, I was pretty freaked out. I mean, I wanted to play a few tricks—not poison someone."

Was it Nancy's imagination, or was Jake actually acting sorry? Maybe they *could* reason with him. It might be their only hope. Even if Tim had already called the police, they wouldn't arrive for another ten minutes or so.

"I didn't mean to set you on fire, either, Nancy," Jake went on in the same contrite tone. "I just thought it would be funny to scare you. In fact, I didn't know you were going to be up there. I was just planning to dump the flour on my stepmother. But you came up on stage, and the fire started, and—and all of a sudden I wasn't a prankster anymore. I mean, who would believe I hadn't known that either the poisoning or the fire was going to happen? Everything kind of—you know—snowballed. I suddenly realized that if I got caught, I was going to go to jail!" He looked appalled.

"That's when I stashed the jar of sweetener in Sam's closet. If the police started looking for evidence, I figured they could have fun trying to pin it on Miss Goody Two-shoes."

"No wonder you wanted me out of the way," Nancy said as sympathetically as she could. "It must have seemed like I was the only person standing between you and your freedom."

He shot Nancy a glance that seemed almost apologetic. "That's right. I didn't want to hurt you. I even kind of liked you. But, of course, I couldn't let you ruin my life, could I?"

"And that's why you lured her to that hole in the floor?" asked George.

"Yup. I hoped that either that or the chisel

142

would finish her off. I have pretty good aim. I play a lot of darts."

Jake stared down at the saw. "This should be pretty foolproof, though," he mused.

Then he looked back up at Nancy. "I've got to hand it to you," he told her. "You caught me fair and square. I wasn't even a strong suspect, was I?"

"No, you—"

"Wait a minute." Jake's voice was suddenly electric with menace. "Speaking of suspects— *where's Tim?"*

Glaring at the girls, he whipped the saw back off its stand.

Uh-oh! thought Nancy hopelessly.

"He sneaked out of here, didn't he? He's going to call the police!" Jake was beginning to scream. "Well, he's not going to get the chance! None of you will ever have a chance again! Say goodbye to one another because— *here goes!"*

Nancy didn't have time to react before he leapt toward the gas pipe.

In the next instant, though, the room was plunged into darkness.

"Hey!" came Jake's furious voice. "What the—"

For a split second Nancy thought that somehow the lights had gone out because Jake had sawed the pipe in two. Then she realized that that couldn't be it.

Tim must have found the circuit breaker! He must have switched off the lights—and the electric saw. That meant all Nancy had to do was—

She hurled herself toward the darkness and smashed full force into Jake. "George! Bess! Over here!" she screamed. "Help me!"

"I'm right behind you," George called back. The three girls yelled that they had pinned him down, and Tim switched the lights back on.

Looking up, Nancy saw Tim was standing in the doorway.

"The police are on their way," he said grimly.

"I know we ought to thank you, Nancy—but I can't make myself feel grateful yet," said Samantha.

It had been an hour since they'd subdued Jake. Samantha and Tim were sitting in the living room with Nancy, Bess, and George. The police had taken Jake away, and Mrs. and Mrs. Tagley left immediately after that to speak with their lawyer.

Amazingly, the other guests were still enjoying the dance. Samantha had made up some excuse for the blackout. And with the music and dancing to distract everyone, they had been able to keep Jake's arrest fairly quiet.

"I can't make myself feel much of anything except sick," Samantha continued. "This is a terrible, terrible tragedy for my family. I—I know Jake isn't my real brother, but he seems like one. I can't forgive myself for thinking that I somehow pushed him into doing this."

"I know you must feel that way," said Nancy sympathetically. "But I don't think anything you did or didn't do made any difference. Once Jake

Sweet Revenge

started to realize the consequences of what he had done, I think he went over the edge."

"Yes, but he would never have had to play those tricks in the first place if he hadn't felt so jealous of me!" Samantha's voice was trembling.

"You did nothing wrong, Sam," Tim said, slipping an arm around her shoulders. "Jake just has very serious problems."

"Oh, Tim, I'm sorry if I've been taking you for granted," Samantha said sadly.

She looked over at Nancy, Bess, and George. "Would you mind leaving us alone for a little while? Tim and I have a lot to talk about. We've had a lot to talk about for a while now."

"Nancy, wait!" Samantha's voice rang out as Nancy, Bess, and George were leaving the dining room the next morning.

Samantha rushed toward them, her white skirt flapping around her legs. She looked much happier. In fact, she looked radiant. And Tim, who was standing behind her in shorts and a polo shirt, was grinning broadly.

"I wanted you three to be the first to know," she said breathlessly. "Tim and I are engaged!"

"What wonderful news!" Nancy said, giving her a warm hug. "When did all this happen?"

"Right after you left us last night," Samantha told her. "We got everything out in the open. My feelings about Brock and my role in the inn, and Tim's role in the inn—"

"And *my* feelings about Brock," said Tim with a chuckle, "which, as you may have guessed, aren't love filled. But Sam convinced me that I really had nothing to worry about."

"I did drag Brock out here all the way from Hollywood," said Samantha. "I didn't think it would be very nice to keep reminding him that I was going out with someone else. But it's all straightened out now."

"I also got Sam to promise not to work so hard," said Tim. "If we're going to get married, I want a wife I can spend time with once in a while."

"Well, you'll get to see me *at* work," Samantha pointed out, taking his hand and squeezing it. "We're going to run the inn together," she explained. "I finally realized that it really is too big a job for me. There's plenty of room for two people at the top—especially two people in love.

"I had a big talk with Mom last night, too," Samantha went on in a rush. "You can't believe how upset she is about what happened. I feel guilty—but she feels even worse."

For an instant her smile wavered. "Mom's not great at leaving things to other people," Samantha added. "But I think that this time she's really going to let me be in charge. She says this whole thing with Jake has changed her priorities."

"Well, that's great," said Bess. "What about Brock?" she added, trying to be casual. "What does he think about all this?"

"I think it's great, too," a deep voice spoke up. None of them had noticed Brock walking up behind Samantha and Tim. He put an arm around Samantha's shoulders and slapped Tim on the back.

"The news about Samantha and Tim, I mean," he clarified. "No one could wish them more happiness than I do."

Then his expression became serious. "And no one could feel sorrier for Jake than I do. I've decided not to press charges, Sam."

"You—you have?" Samantha stammered.

Brock nodded. "Jake needs a lot of help. As long as he gets it, I'm not going to hold a grudge. There's been too much of that already. It's time to move on."

"Speaking of moving on," asked George, "what's happening with the festival?"

Samantha giggled. "I'll have to make sure not to forget about it, won't I? Today should be pretty easy. Five guest chefs are giving workshops. Do any of you want to come?"

Nancy and her friends looked at one another for a few seconds. "You know, I don't think so," Nancy said at last. "I feel as though it's time to head home." Her friends nodded in agreement.

"Oh, that will never do," said Brock promptly. A mischievous light was dancing in his dazzling blue eyes. "I'm leaving for home tomorrow myself. We can't let everything fizzle out this way."

He smiled down at Bess. "So, Bess, would you do me the honor of accompanying me to a movie this afternoon?"

* * *
147

"He's coming in five minutes! *Five more minutes!*" caroled Bess, dancing around the living room of the girls' suite.

From where she lay stretched out on the sofa, Nancy looked up at her friend. Bess was wearing a pink minidress that showed off her curvy figure perfectly. And her excitement had brought a flush to her cheeks that only added to her appeal. Brock Sawyer, look out!

"Calm down," said George. "You'll fall and break your leg, and then Brock will have to take *you* to the hospital instead of the movies."

Bess flopped down into a chair. "Wouldn't you guys like to finish my packing for me? When I come back, I *know* I won't feel like it."

"Forget it," Nancy told her. "I've got enough problems with my own suitcase. Why is it that the stuff you take home always takes up three times more space than the stuff you brought with you?"

"Oh, all right. I'll do it myself later." Suddenly Bess brightened. "After all, I may have to tuck in some little present. Brock might be feeling sentimental—you never know."

"Maybe he'll even give you a nice, big box of chocolates," said George. "Something that will *really* make you remember this trip."

"No way," said Bess immediately. "You guys aren't going to believe this, but I've had enough chocolate to last me the rest of my life."

Nancy grinned. "You know, Bess, I do believe you," she said. "I don't want to go near chocolate for a long, long time. But I'm glad this case had a sweet ending after all."

Nancy's next case:

A is for Arson, B is for Bribery, C is for Computer fraud . . . and D is for Danger when Nancy goes undercover to investigate a grade-changing scheme at Brewster Academy. Someone has penetrated the school's computer and is extorting cash from students in exchange for upgrading their academic records. But now Nancy's messing with the program, and the mystery hacker is determined to make *her* pay.

The school is abuzz with controversy, and Nancy's in the middle of it. Just about everyone, from a jealous girlfriend to an angry administration, is looking to take a byte out of her. But Nancy's most dangerous enemy of all is sitting at a computer keyboard—and she's about to make a shocking discovery that could be terminal . . . in *EASY MARKS*, Case #62 in The Nancy Drew Files™.

Forthcoming titles in the Nancy Drew Files ™ Series